Alaina had never been kissed before and at first she wasn't sure she liked it, but then, as his tongue touched her lips, coaxing, delicately exploring, almost tormentingly gentle, she forgot her fear and started imitating his actions, kissing him back. Her arms came around his neck and that's when his kiss changed from gentle to demanding, devouring, stealing her breath away, and making her head feel drugged. Alaina felt lost in a stream of emotions, her body reacting without her permission. She felt herself answering his kisses and molding her body into his. His kisses trailed down her neck toward her breast, and she felt her head swirling.

What was he doing to her? It must stop. She didn't want him to stop. She didn't know what she should do and before she could stop herself, she whispered, "Please!"

Alexander stopped instantly. He had seen the limitless empathy in her eyes and that had been his undoing. Here this young woman had lost everything in one day and yet was reaching out to him, to comfort him—a purely unselfish act. He wanted to kiss her inviting lips, to crush her body to his and take away the pain he knew she was feeling, a pain he understood all too well.

To
Pam &
Mark,
I hope you like
the characters & the
story - let me know
I enjoy your email
messages -
Keep
writing

# Sands & Shores

*by*

Samantha Kingsley

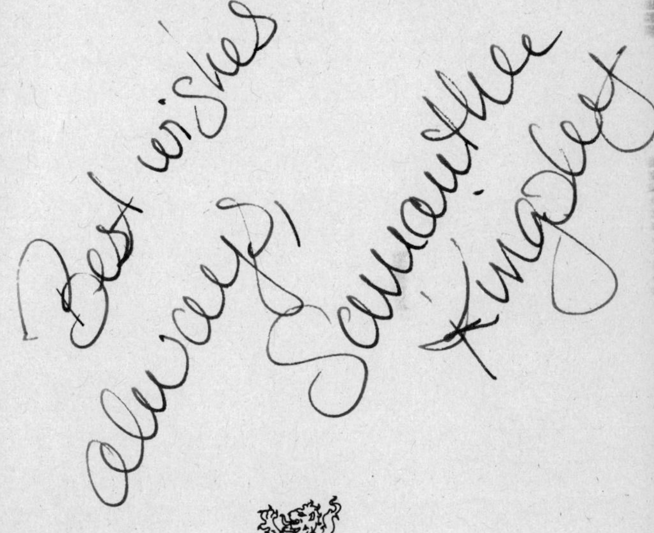

Commonwealth
Publications

A Commonwealth Publications Paperback
SANDS & SHORES

This edition published 1996
by Commonwealth Publications
9764 - 45th Avenue,
Edmonton, AB, CANADA T6E 5C5


ISBN: 1-55197-126-7



Designed by: Federico Caceres

Printed in Canada

*Dedication*

*In memory of my father, Werner Luloh*

# Foreword

In times past, desert nomads considered the horse to be a gift of the gods, a combination of wind and flame. The Arabian mare was considered a member of the household, not just a beast of burden; she slept beside her master in his tent and was trained as a watchdog. Yet the Arabian's first and most important characteristic is his prepotency, his ability to pass his traits onto his descendants. Every thoroughbred today traces its lines back to an Arabian. There are very few completely pure Arabian horses in Arabia today, and none have ever been sold.

Today in the Kingdom of Saudi Arabia, the population is approximately 14 million. The language is Arabic, although English is widely spoken. Muslims' lives are guided by the Koran, the holy book of Islam. There is no separation of religion and state, and in the Koran it is lawful for a man to marry up to four wives. Through the wealth of oil production, much has changed in this country, but one can still find desert nomads....

# Prologue

**Meadow Creek Ranch, Wyoming**

**1980**

The butler of the large mansion sat in the large foyer, warily watching the closed door of the downstairs den where his wife waited on his employer. The door of the den opened and his wife hurried out, carrying a tray of untouched food. Her eyes were tired and red, and her checks showed smudges of tears having been wiped off earlier. "How is the lad?" the butler asked his wife.

"Oh, Martin, he hasn't eaten anything in days and he just sits there, staring into the fire, not saying a word. He looks so hard and untouchable, it scares me. At least when he lost Rebecca he cried."

Martin stood up, took the tray out of his wife's hands, put it down on the eighteenth century chair, and took her into his arms. "It's all so cruel and unfair! He's only twenty years old," she cried.

"Life isn't fair, Clara," he said, trying to console her with one of his many clichés.

Clara pulled away from her husband. "Why did Rebecca have to break his heart and move away? Then he wouldn't have gotten mixed up with that woman. I can't even say her name, I'm so angry!"

"Now, Clara. They were both only sixteen and her father had the right to take his daughter and move away."

"But it hurt him so deeply!"

"I agree. I myself thought it was a passing infatuation, but you were right, Devon really did love the girl."

"And besides, it was a stupid reason, if I do say so. It was just an excuse. Her father took her away saying she was too young, but only a few months later she married some distant relative in Italy! I can't believe she wanted that—I could see she loved Devon."

"Clara, you have to let it go, just as Devon has to." He took her into his arms again.

She stayed there only a moment and then pushed him away again. "I have to go see how Susan is doing. I finally got her to go to bed a few hours ago. She might be hungry now."

Martin took his wife's hands. "We have each other and I will never leave you."

Clara managed a smile for a brief moment and wiped her tears away with the back of her hand. "I wish I could say the same thing for Susan and Devon. In many ways I'm happy we don't have money; it's brought them nothing but unhappiness."

"Tell Susan not to worry about the ranch. Everyone is pitching in extra hard right now, and if she needs anything..."

"She knows, Martin, but I'll tell her."

Clara made her way up the long winding stairway to the second floor, past the twenty beautiful bedrooms in the manor, and stood outside the bedroom Susan had shared with her husband. When her husband had disappeared with the family fortune a few months ago, Susan had never shed a tear, just like her son, Devon. But this latest tragedy had torn her apart.

Clara opened the door of Susan's bedroom and quietly walked in, but stayed close by the door. The large canopied cherry wood bed was empty. Susan stood by the window staring out into the night. Without looking at Clara, Susan said softly, "Come in, Clara."

Clara wrung her hands and looked at the woman who had hired her twenty years earlier. Susan had found her on the streets of Cheyenne, begging for food. She had paid off her debts, cleaned her up and given her employment, and most memorably, she had given her a wonderful wedding when she and Martin had married thirteen years ago. All the employees loved Susan because she had always treated them as family; now they were willing to ride out the bad times with her.

"Is there any change in Devon?"

Clara shook her head as Susan turned around to look at her.

"What can I say to Devon? His first love is taken away from him because her father says our lives are too different, both in money and social status, and now Devon's wife leaves him because we are no longer wealthy." She sighed heavily.

"She was no good, Susan, you knew it from the moment you laid eyes on her."

"Yes, but they were married and I was going to support their decision. I didn't think she could be so terribly cruel." She sighed again and added softly, "At least she confessed in the end."

"Confessed?"

Susan looked out the window again. "The baby wasn't Devon's."

Clara inhaled so sharply Susan quickly turned back to look at her. "But that's why Devon married her in the first place!" Clara said.

"Worse yet, the baby's father was Devon's best friend. She found out how much money Devon stood to inherit, broke up with the father of her baby without telling him she was pregnant, and played on Devon's emotions, knowing he still wasn't over Rebecca. She was after our money and she would have done anything to get it. This may be terrible, but I'm glad she's out of his life, leaving no ties, although I know Devon blames himself for the baby's death."

Clara shook her head. "But it wasn't his fault! She threw herself down those stairs when he wouldn't pay for an abortion."

Clara nodded. "I'm hoping time will heal all things. In the meantime, I think Devon needs to get away for a while. I have some relatives in Spain he could visit."

"If you need some money..."

"Thank you, Clara. We really are all right."

"Everyone on the ranch wants me to let you and Devon know we are there for you."

"And somehow we'll make it together; no one will have to leave the ranch. We'll sell off some of the horses. I've spoken with our lawyers and they feel we can save the ranch by mortgaging it. The ranch was the only thing George wasn't able to touch."

Susan hadn't spoken of her husband since he had left. He had taken all the money he could liquidate quickly, emptying all their bank accounts and cashing in their bonds and CDs only two months after Susan's father died, leaving everything to Susan. Unfortunately, her husband had joint signing power on everything. Susan had told Clara that she believed he was probably somewhere in South America living on the millions her father had worked a lifetime to amass. "Have the lawyers heard from Mr. Maxwell?" Clara asked softly.

"No. I don't think anyone ever will hear from George again. In one way, I'm glad it all happened. Now Devon is free and he will get on with his life, just as I have. One shouldn't have to live out their life in a loveless relationship, but I know Devon, and he would have, just as I did." She suddenly straightened her slim, tall body, and appeared years younger again, resembling the striking young woman that had once lived happily in this house. "I'm going down to talk to Devon. We can all start over and do things differently this time."

Clara followed Susan at a distance and watched as she went downstairs to the den and then hesitate as she was about to knock. Instead of knocking, she opened the door to the den and walked in, leaving the door open behind her.

The fire was dying and her son was sitting in her father's chair, bent over with his elbows leaning on his legs and his head resting in his opened hands. She walked with her hand outstretched as if to comfort her son, but as she walked by the desk, she saw a book, her father's diary, lying open. She walked behind the desk instead.

"Everything is a lie," Devon said suddenly, startling her.

"What do you mean?"

Devon looked up at his mother, his eyes cold and hard. "I mean my grandfather paid Rebecca's father one million dollars to disappear and make sure Rebecca and I never found each other."

"What are you talking about?" Susan asked, sounding defensive of her father.

"Read it for yourself. It's right there in his diary. It was all for some promise given years ago that one day two families would be tied by blood. Not only did grandfather want our horses' blood to mingle, but he wanted his children's blood to mingle with theirs as well."

"With the sheik?"

"It'll never happen!" Devon vowed. "Even with Rebecca out of the picture and married to someone else..."

"But if it's true that Rebecca..."

"Rebecca is out of my life," Devon said, standing up, "But Grandfather will never get his wish. In his diary I found a letter, dated only a month before grandfather's death, from the sheik in Arabia, and it might be an answer to our financial problems. There is a horse in the desert that the sheik wanted to give grandfather. It must be something special. I'm going there at the end of the week to bring that horse back, and I will get back the money father took." There was icy bitterness in the young man's voice. "There is no loyalty, especially not in this family..."

Susan had picked up the diary, but now dropped it as if it had bitten her hand, and walked out of the office. She stopped before Martin and Clara. "My father could be ruthless. Maybe later I can reason with Devon, maybe not, but you heard he's planning on going to the desert, just as my father did many times. Martin, you know what he'll need. Make sure he's well prepared."

She started up the long stairway and Clara started up after her, but Martin stopped her. "She's hurting. Let her be. You heard what the diary said—James paid off Rebecca's father."

"I can't believe he would do that!"

"I've been in this family a long time and he didn't make all his money being nice all the time.

You might have seen him as a generous, kind man, but he knew well the power his money gave him. He's hurt his own grandson, the one he loved the most, maybe beyond repair. Susan understands that."

"What's all this about blood ties?"

"Where do you think all those beautiful horses came from? It's an old promise made many years ago between James and a sheik in Arabia. Every so many years, when a special horse came along, they would give it as a gift to each other as a means of expressing a friendship that went deeper than brothers. The way I heard it was, James saved the sheik's life once, and vice versa."

"And they wanted their children to marry?"

"They both had only daughters and so they decided to wait for their grandchildren."

"Does the sheik have grandchildren?" Clara asked.

"Not that I'm aware of. And you heard the lad, knowing what he knows now, James ruined any hopes of that ever happening. Devon will never have anything to do with that. But there is a large part of Devon that is just like his grandfather, and he will make use of his grandfather's friendship overseas. I have no doubt that he will get back what his father lost."

"I'm afraid for him, Martin."

"He'll be all right, Clara. There's courage and fire in his blood. I know. I know the family history."

# Chapter 1

**New York**

**September 2, 1992**

Joe, chauffeur and bodyguard, entered Alexander's office with a smile on his face and a paper in his hand, and Alexander knew instantly Joe fully intended to bore him with this week's tabloid column, which Alexander already knew stated he had romanced royalty on his latest business trip to Italy. Joe's smile faded as Alexander looked up briefly from his financial report, his dark brows drawn in a slight frown over his intense blue eyes.

At thirty-two, Alexander had acquired an uncompromising strength of character and body, his very presence exuding an aura of power, every feature of his sun-darkened face stamped with authority—something most women found sexually appealing, but most men found disturbingly uncomfortable.

"Troubles, boss?" Joe asked.

"It seems I need to clear up a situation in Saudi for Devon Maxwell right away."

Most people knew Devon Maxwell as a rich, reclusive man from Wyoming who owned a vast amount of real-estate world-wide and had an unknown amount of money in bank accounts in Switzerland and the Cayman Islands along with many assets under Maxwell Enterprises. And since Alexander McClyde was President of Maxwell Enterprises, Joe found himself also indirectly employed by Devon Maxwell.

"What do you mean by situation?" Joe asked, his interest peaked.

"Just what I said. I'm headed for Saudi Arabia. Take a couple of weeks paid vacation, Joe. I'm going to visit a few friends while I'm there."

"When are you leaving?"

"I'm just waiting for a couple of horses to be flown from the Maxwell ranch in Wyoming to New York as a gift to a sheik there, and should be leaving this evening. Since Martha's going to be busy taking memos from me for the next few hours, could you make sure the company jet will be ready by seven?"

"Sure." Then more quietly, Joe mumbled as he left the room, "Another vacation. I'd rather go along, where the action is."

SAUDI ARABIA

Alaina sat on the bed next to her ill foster mother, Zainab. She was dying of cancer and there was nothing anyone could do for her. She had not wanted to stay in the hospital, so Alaina had made sure she could come home to the warm yellow-painted walls that she knew so well.

Silent tears ran down Alaina's face. There was no one else that loved her as much as the woman who now was fading away, and Alaina loved her as no one else did. Zainab mattered little to her husband or his family because she had not borne him any sons; she had not borne any children for her husband.

When Alaina was six, she and her birth family had been taking a cruise on the Mediterranean. A terrible storm had broken out, unusual for those waters, and the cruise ship had started to sink. She was saved by a young man who had thrown her from the sinking ship and helped her float ashore with him. That was twelve years ago, and Alaina had come to live with Ahmeed bin Ahmad Al Sudairi and Zainab, his first and only wife at that time.

Not having any children of her own, the young Zainab had immediately become attached to the young child. Ahmeed had little use for girls, especially those not of his own blood, but was wealthy enough to allow his young wife the luxury of keeping the young child. Unlike many men, Ahmeed never divorced Zainab, having great respect for Zainab's father, Abdul. Instead, over time, he had taken three other wives who gave him sons and daughters.

Alaina heard voices outside the room. She quietly got up and hurried along the hallway to peek through the balcony and listen to the men in the large sitting room below.

Her foster father was there with his brother and several men she recognized as the Mutawa, the Morals Police of Islam. There was also another man they addressed as Mustafa, whom she guessed was the same age as her father, and was now talking in a voice so low that she could not hear what he said. She instinctively disliked all the men below. She heard her mother's name mentioned and then one of the Mutawa pulled out a letter and handed it to her father.

"It is addressed to Devon Maxwell in America. Why is your wife writing letters to a man in America?" the Mutawa wanted to know. "She has shamed you."

Ahmeed took time to read the letter. "I have never seen this letter. I don't understand this."

"It is forbidden for your daughter to marry a non-Muslim," the Mutawa reminded her father.

"She is not my blood. I do not care whom she marries."

Alaina sucked in her breath. She knew her father did not love her, but that he cared nothing for her at all made her tremble. How could he be so cold?

"She has been adopted into the Muslim life. I will take her off your hands. I will marry her," the man named Mustafa said.

Alaina felt sure that under different circumstances, Ahmeed would have taken the time to consider the situation, but with the Mutawa in his house and with the shame of his ailing wife on him, she watched in horror as he nodded.

"If it would please you?" he asked the men of the Mutawa.

They seemed satisfied with the outcome. "Your wife must be punished."

"My wife is dying," he said, and Alaina thought she detected a slight sadness in his voice. Or had she just wished it there?

"She must be punished for the shame she has brought you."

Alaina ran back to her mother. She would not allow her to be punished. She was dying. She had heard of the punishments carried out on women who had shamed their families—drowning, stoning to death, flogging and other forms of cruel punishment.

Alaina would not let them take her mother now. She would die with dignity. Maybe she could sneak her out through the back and ride away with her, maybe to the city of Jeddah where her mother had family, family who accepted her.

Alaina had always been the outcast in the household of Ahmeed. In the beginning, before the other children were born, she had tried desperately to get her adoptive father's attention, but failed miserably. Other children had come along, but only the males seemed to matter to Ahmeed. The only time Alaina seemed to fit in was when she would journey with Zainab to see her family in Jeddah. They were different and allowed her to ride horses and be part of their family, even though her blue eyes and blond hair set her apart from the rest of them.

Not until she became a woman three years ago with the appearance of her first menses did she seem to fit in, for it was then that she received her first veil and abaaya which hid her features from the rest of the world. But it was around that time that Zainab first became ill. Alaina traveled with her mother to Madinah for medical treatments and only when she was alone with her mother in the hospital room did she remove her heavy veil.

It was a week now since they had arrived back from their last trip to the hospital. Alaina was angry with her foster father's inattentiveness to Zainab and stayed in the woman's quarters or in her mother's room at all times. She also knew Ahmeed was already planning his next marriage, to a woman her own age, as soon as her beloved mother died.

She patted her mother's hand. "Mother, please wake up."

Tired eyes opened and the once exceptionally beautiful woman tried to smile. "What is it child?"

"There are men downstairs that say you wrote a letter to a man in America. Is that true?"

Zainab did not look surprised. "I have written to the man who once saved your life and brought you to me. Now he must save you again."

"But father has your letter."

"I sent several letters to make sure at least one would be delivered. I gave two to the British nurse in the hospital." She sighed and Alaina could see her pain. "Marry this man, Alaina. Devon Maxwell is a good friend to my father and is a good man. I know that he still lives in your heart."

"Oh, mother, they want to punish you. I must get you out of here!"

"No, daughter. They will punish you, if you do. Wait for Devon Maxwell. He will come for you."

"But he's not here and the Mutawa are downstairs now. We must go." Her mother only shook her head and closed her eyes. "Please," Alaina pleaded. She tried to pick up her mother and carry her, but she heard footsteps coming upstairs into the woman's quarters.

Alaina looked around her for a weapon to protect her mother. She saw an ancient jeweled sword hanging on the wall, a gift from her mother's mother on her wedding day. It was only fitting that it now protect her life. Alaina pulled it off the wall, but had to drag it behind her to the door since it was nearly as heavy as she was. Then she stood waiting, holding it, ready to strike.

She looked at her weak mother, and smiled bravely to give her mother some courage, though not feeling much herself. Somewhere in the back of her mind she remembered being separated from her first mother, and although that memory was very dim, it now weighed heavily on her actions.

Suddenly the door flew open forcefully and Alaina jumped back. The large man named Mustafa entered through the door with a look in his eyes that promised violence. He caught sight of Alaina holding the sword and an amused smile slowly appeared on his dark face. He stopped the man pushing up behind him. "I'll handle this," he said and slowly approached Alaina.

Alaina stood determined and ready to strike, but before she could swing the heavy sword, the Arab grabbed it from her and secured her hands behind her back. Quickly he removed the rope holding the privacy drapery over her mother's bed and tied it tightly around her small hands. He laughed loudly as she fought like a trapped wild animal while he shoved her toward the door.

But his laughter turned into a shout of agony. He whirled upon the older woman who was barely able to stand before him and whose face was now drained of all color. As weak as she was, she had managed to pierce a small dagger into the man's shoulder. He kicked her brutally, sending her flying against the end of the bed.

Alaina cried out and started toward the woman crumpled on the floor, but Mustafa grabbed her arm and yanked her back to him. She let out a small cry and struggled to free herself, but it was hopeless.

"The woman is dead, let us go," he growled, shoving her in front of him.

Finally he stopped pushing her as they reached the large sitting room downstairs, where her father and the men of the Mutawa waited. He flung her to the ground in front of them.

Alaina sat very still with her eyes turned to the ground in subjection, yet inside she felt total rebellion. How unfair life was for women in the desert. Now she was at the mercy of these men, who looked down at her in contempt.

The men were still speaking of what had happened in the room upstairs. Suddenly, her head whirled as her father's hand struck her cheek. She looked up and stared angrily back at this man who would allow her ailing mother to be punished, feeling hostility with a vehemence she had not known she possessed.

Her father hit her again and this time the man holding her hair pulled her up. "She is mine now. I will take care of any punishment to be given." Mustafa looked at the Mutawa and asked, "Are you satisfied with the situation?" They nodded their agreement and Mustafa announced, "Then we shall leave this household."

Once outside the house, Mustafa turned toward Alaina and she could feel his black eyes as they looked over her body, as if he could touch her with them. A wicked smile appeared on his face and Alaina shivered at the cruelty in his gaze. But she did not blink as she looked back into his small black eyes, nor did her slender body move. She hoped he would not notice she was shuddering.

"So, you are Alaina," he said. "I have heard many things about you." He rubbed her hair between his fingers as he spoke. "Your eyes are indeed the color belonging to a witch, blue as the sea, and your hair the color of the sun. They also say while you speak our language, you are like no woman of ours, and no man has touched you." He lowered his face to hers. "We shall see."

Alaina's stomach churned with nausea that swept over her from his sweaty smell and the blood on his shirt, which reminded her of her dying mother who no one cared about. Tears didn't come. Instead, the anger of the injustice overflowed.

"You pig," she said, keeping her voice low so as not to give away any quiver. "You will regret this. I will avenge my mother."

The Arab laughed. "You are an undisciplined one. Abdul has spoiled you with many freedoms, but that will end now. You will come to know subjection and obedience as becomes a woman." He paused and looked her over carefully before adding, "And be domesticated."

He pulled strongly on her hair again, forcing her close to his face. Alaina felt chills in her soul and uttered, "Never." Then with all the force she could muster, she spit in his face.

The Arab's eyes widened with wrath and he swung back his hand and hit her across the face with such force that she flew to the ground. He raised his hand, ready to strike her again, but as Alaina turned to stare back at him, unmoving, he seemed to change his mind. An ugly smile came to his lips again. "A challenge, how amusing. We shall see, my princess."

As the sun began to sink on the horizon, he turned to his men and shouted orders to mount up. "Come, it is time to go to your new home. Put these on." He handed her a veil and an abaaya.

He freed her hands and as soon as Alaina finished putting on the garments, she felt herself lifted up onto a waiting horse. She began to wonder what kind of life she would be forced to live now. Was he a tent dweller as his horses and camels suggested? Was a tent to be her new home—or would she even live beyond this day?

Mustafa mounted in front of Alaina, forcing her onto the horse's haunches. Had it not been for her excellent horsemanship, she would have fallen off as soon as the horse started galloping.

Numbed by the events of the past few minutes, which seemed more like hours, her mind returned to a different time in her life, when she was near death, and a stranger had helped her and brought her to this land. She thought about the handsome young man, with the same color hair as hers, the stranger Devon Maxwell that had saved her from the sea. If one could fall in love at six, she had. She knew by heart the words to a poem he had written in a fairy tale book many years ago. And how appropriate some of the words seemed now, *Though time be fleet and I and thou are half a life asunder*...but he was too far away to help her now.

In the past, when things had gone wrong, or the children of the village had teased her about her different appearance, she would warn them that she had been saved by a wonderful prince, and that one day he would come and take her away to his beautiful castle, where she would be a queen and live happily ever after, while they would remain where they were. As she got older, she realized castles weren't being built any more, and princes didn't rescue damsels in distress, but somehow she still clung to the hope that Devon Maxwell would come to her rescue again.

She squared her shoulders and lifted her chin, letting the wind dry her tears. She would not allow herself to give up nor give in to these men. She would be strong and avenge her mother. She thought of the blood that flowed through her veins and the stories Zainab's father had told her about her native people, the Vikings. How they were warriors and needed to die in battle to enter their heaven, Valhalla. All she knew of her past was that she had lived in Sweden with her family who had drowned on their cruise on the Mediterranean. Only she had been spared. Then it had been a storm at sea that had taken her mother, now it was these men who had taken another mother away.

Alaina started to shiver as it became dark and shadows began to fade, bringing with it a drastic drop in temperature. She tried to position her body behind the Arab's without touching him yet out of the wind, but they were riding at a fast pace.

Alaina heard a horseman come riding up from her rear shouting, "Mustafa! Someone is following. Only one rider."

"Take care of him," Mustafa commanded. The two men riding closest to them turned from the group and headed back toward the rider.

Alaina wondered who would have followed them. Had her father changed his mind? Had her mother's father, Abdul, come for her? Yet there was little hope in her heart because she knew as a woman she did not matter enough for anyone to challenge Mustafa and the Mutawa.

# Chapter 2

With his great stallion, Pegasus, beneath him racing across the desert sands, Alexander once again felt adrenaline flowing through his veins and the restlessness he continually had to suppress in New York subsided. Only twenty-four hours ago he'd been reading the latest financial report of a new acquisition for Maxwell Enterprises in an office overlooking Manhattan.

He had slept during the nine-hour flight which had landed him in Riyadh and then a half hour later he had landed again outside Jeddah. He had been greeted at the plane by his friend Abdul, who brought news of his daughter Zainab's death and her beloved adopted daughter's abduction by Mustafa.

Alexander had wasted no time. Mustafa had a two hour head start on him. He unloaded his gift to Abdul, a beautiful filly, the product of years of breeding between Devon Maxwell's family and the sheik's. Next, he unloaded his powerful stallion. He allowed the stallion to run the kinks out of his legs as he changed into clothes supplied by Abdul, while Abdul packed other necessities for his journey across the desert. Alexander had been in the desert before. He had stayed with Abdul for over a year once, learning much about the ways of the desert and how to survive here.

Now, only hours later, he would soon meet up with Mustafa and the young woman, Alaina. His face relaxed, but not his dark eyes. They had a wariness about them that never eased. He patted Pegasus' neck. He had pushed him hard to catch up to Mustafa, and he now was wet with sweat.

Alexander saw his opponents before they could see him. For this very reason, he had dressed himself in black. He was ready for them. He pulled his stallion to a dead stop and stood silently waiting, nearly invisible in the blackness of the night. The large horse shook his head wildly and pawed the ground. He trembled as he stood waiting. This is what he was bred for: the race, the battle.

As the two riders were nearly upon him, Alexander urged his stallion into a leaping bound, crashing into one horseman, throwing him from his horse and sending his rifle to the sand, while the other rider turned toward him, gun drawn. Pegasus reared and released an ear-shattering scream that filled the air. The oncoming horse sidestepped out of the stallion's path, throwing its rider off balance. Alexander moved forward, striking the rider down. By then, the first rider had scrambled onto his horse and started riding back to the others. Alexander urged his horse forward and quickly overtook the rider, sending him from his mount.

"Sorry, I want to stay a surprise," he said, and continued in pursuit until he could see Mustafa's group ahead of him. He counted maybe twenty-five men, and knew he could never take on all of them. Nor could he count on what Mustafa would do next.

He remembered his last meeting with Mustafa

all too well. He straightened his back and could almost feel the scars against his shirt, whip lashes administered by Mustafa himself. But that was ten years ago. Since that meeting, he had trained with the sword and in the martial arts with a fortitude and voracity that most men only dreamed of. It had strengthened his body and given equanimity to his soul. Now he had come back with added years of maturity that had only served to harden him, making him a dangerous man to reckon with.

Alexander heard a man shout, "Only one rider coming, Mustafa, and it is not one of us."

Alexander could see the men on their horses now and could see that one man carried with him another rider, a child...no, a woman. He watched as the rider pulled up his horse and looked back. They all came to a stop. It was very dark and with no moon, Mustafa would have a hard time seeing who he was.

"Quiet!" Mustafa commanded. The only sound to be heard in the desert night was the pounding stride of a tremendous animal. "Only one horse is capable of such speed and such strength. Alexander and Pegasus are back!"

Alexander himself came to a stop just outside Mustafa's little group. Mustafa pulled Alaina off his horse. "Here, take this woman," he said, roughly handing her over to the nearest man, "but do not touch her, she is mine." Then he added in a warning tone, "Anyone touches her, I will cut off his hand."

Alexander watched and waited for Mustafa. Pegasus was pulling at the bit, not wanting to stop, eager to continue the battle. But Mustafa was coming alone. *Damn, he is so unpredictable*, Alexander thought. Mustafa drew closer and shouted, "Alexander, my brother, you are back!"

One of Alexander's dark eyebrow lifted slightly at hearing himself being called "brother." What was Mustafa's game now? There was not even friendship between the two, much less feelings of brotherhood. Mustafa's father had tried to steal Pegasus from Abdul and Alexander, and had lost his eldest son in doing so, the stallion trampling him to death. Mustafa's father had sworn revenge on Alexander, but Alexander had left the country, taking Pegasus with him.

Mustafa reigned in his horse directly beside Alexander. "Mustafa, it's been a long time," Alexander responded.

"Too long, my brother. My father would have liked to have seen you again. He had great respect for you. Please understand, I do not hold the death of my brother against you any longer. Let there be peace. Come with us, to our home, as my brother."

Alexander knew to have a chance at saving the girl, he needed to play along right now. He knew Mustafa hated him, and he would have to quickly figure out the rules to this game—if there were any.

Alexander watched the other men intently as he rode in among them. He was alert to anyone who might strike at him or Pegasus, but showed no emotion. Some of the men showed their wonder, for they had heard of Pegasus and the man that had tamed him. Others were only distantly interested. Alexander saw the woman, but could not tell through the dark veil who it was.

Mustafa grabbed Alaina around the waist, set her in front of him and briefed his men, "This is Alexander, our friend. Let us go!"

Alaina had hated sitting behind the Arab, but now sitting in front of him was pure torment. She hated his arms around her, his legs next to hers and the sound of his breath in her ear. She felt another wave of sickness wash over her and forced herself to keep her mind concentrated on other things.

She knew there wasn't much she could do now to escape, but maybe once they reached their destination, she could start some kind of commotion, free a horse or camel and slip out unnoticed.

She wondered about the man that had joined them. He was Mustafa's friend and maybe even more dangerous, judging by his size alone, yet maybe she could use him to cause a diversion somehow. She looked in his direction again and saw his horse was truly magnificent, never had she seen such a broad chest and long powerful legs. She tried to see more of the horse, but when she raised her eyes, she saw the man was watching her. She looked away quickly, but not before noticing his eyes. Her heart started pounding quickly—were they blue, like her own?

Her adopted grandfather had often received visitors from the western world who had bought oil and brought presents. She was never allowed to visit with them, none of the women were, but she had always wanted to see if any were like her, with blond hair or blue eyes. Could this be a visitor from the West? Alexander was not an Arabic name, yet Mustafa had called him brother; surely that could not be.

The horses slowed and she saw fires burning and tents pitched in the immediate distance. She wondered if this was where Mustafa lived. She had at least hoped for a house.

They stopped and Mustafa pulled Alaina off his horse. As the men dispersed, Mustafa dragged Alaina toward a tent and pushed her inside. There was no one inside and Alaina looked out of the tent to get a better view of the camp. She watched as Mustafa walked back to Alexander and heard him give him his orders. "I will be back later, don't go anywhere," he said laughing in the way Alaina had come to hate. "I would ask you to share this tent, but instead I give you mine, right over there," he pointed. "Make yourself at home."

"Mustafa, the woman you have in your tent, I have promised to take care of."

"I do not honor any promises by other men." The Arab smiled, but his voice carried no humor.

"But I am bound by mine. Do we fight over her?"

"I do not fight over a woman. She is mine now, and I intend to keep her."

"I will fight for her," Alexander said loudly enough for all to hear, and watched as men came out of their tents. "Shall we test our skill?" He pulled out his sword. "Winner gets the girl."

Mustafa scowled. He had been challenged and his men were watching. They expected a fight now. "To the death then, my friend," he said, pulling out his sword. "The woman can wait."

Alaina looked out of the tent and saw the two men face each other with drawn swords. She wondered why they did not shoot each other with their guns, but only thought about it fleetingly, since this was her moment to escape. She might not get another. She waited until she heard the clinging of metal striking metal. She found a horse nearby. She felt its sweat and heaving sides and wished she could have found a fresh mount, but she had no choice. She could feel her heart beating through her entire body, and her hand trembled slightly as she gathered the reins. She was stealing a horse, a crime punishable by death! But while the thought of stealing upset her, as she kicked the horses' sides, she felt exhilarated at the same time. It had been too long since she had ridden a horse, and if she was going to die, this was the way she wanted to die.

Alexander saw her galloping off first. He dodged the sword coming at him and whistled for his stallion. Man and horse ran toward each other.

"You coward!" Mustafa shouted after Alexander. Then he, too, saw the girl galloping off. He shouted to the men, "After them! Kill him, but do not harm the girl!"

Alaina heard a horseman coming up behind her, and her heart started beating brutally against her chest as she saw the large stranger racing toward her, gaining ground quickly. All she could do was urge her already tired horse on. She hoped her determination was enough to hold up her exhausted horse.

The large figure moved in closer and Alaina felt a powerful arm come around her, pulling her off her horse and onto the immense stallion just as her horse stumbled. "Hang on," the man said in her ear.

The voice was resonant and not frightening. She felt the hardness of the man's thighs around her and felt incredibly small between his broad shoulders. Beneath her, she felt tremendous muscles catapulting as the man communicated his urgency to his stallion and they seemed to almost fly above the sand. The wind whipped wildly in her face and her eyes started tearing. How could this man see where they were going? Never had she gone so fast!

# Chapter 3

After what seemed an eternity of riding at an incredible speed, Alaina finally felt the stallion slow his pace. Her eyes were still burning and tears ran down her cheeks, making it hard to see where they were going, but she was able to see a cave ahead.

The stallion trotted inside. "Where are we?"

"Shhhh," Alexander commanded. "This place echoes and they'll hear us, if we haven't lost them."

How could he have found this place in the night? Had he been here before? Why was he hiding her from Mustafa?

"Who are you?" she whispered, trying to turn around and see her captor. But he wouldn't let her, his strong arms held her tightly against him as his upper body pressed down on hers. She saw the ceiling was becoming lower as they rode deeper into the cavern, and her captor had to bend down to keep from hitting his head. She tried struggling again, but soon realized she was wasting her strength.

"If you promise to be quiet and sit still, I'll release you."

She didn't answer and remained quiet. This man was not a relative, nor a Muslim, and by his actions, he had violated her just as much as Mustafa. She would not be kept against her will by this man either. She had no intention of being dragged from one man to the next.

The moment his arms left her and she felt him relax slightly, she eyed the knife she saw in his boot. It was the only chance she had. She grabbed the knife with lightning quickness and closed her eyes as she stabbed his thigh before he could react. Then quickly, she tried to throw herself off the horse. But her captor's solid, strong arm encircled her again and a hand covered her mouth to prevent her from screaming.

"Get off," he whispered gruffly in her ear. He pulled her down with him, and before she could think of causing any further incidents, she was bound and gagged and sitting on the ground. Now she felt truly trapped, without chance of escape—surely he would kill her.

He took down his saddle bag and then examined the wound. Quickly, he extracted the knife and put pressure on his leg as blood quickly stained his pants. Alaina felt a shudder go through her. Never had she deliberately hurt anyone, and now she had stabbed this stranger who might very well kill her for it. How she hated this man—all of them!

How had her mother ever been able to stand her life? Alaina always thought she wanted to be more like her mother, who was humble and meek, for things might have been easier that way. She had always striven to be more like her, but now, thinking about her mother brought tears to her eyes. Why was she thinking of this now? She tried hard to think of something else and to hide her tears from her enemy, yet she didn't dare take her eyes off of him either.

She knew he watched her also, through his peripheral vision, as he took supplies out of the first aid kit. Blood had soaked through his pant leg, and he began to tear his pants to see what had to be done. He stopped and turned his attention to Alaina and wearily asked, "Did you learn stitching from your mother?"

Alaina looked at him defiantly, but her courage failed her slightly as she looked into his eyes. She realized they were dark blue, a very angry dark blue. She nodded hesitantly.

"Good," Alexander said, getting up and limping over to her. Alaina didn't know what he was going to do. She lurched back and tried to shrink into the wall behind her. "I'm not going to hit you, but if you pull a stunt like this again, I can't vouch for what I'll do to you. Do you understand?" He demanded her acknowledgment before he untied her. He sat back down, leaned back against the wall of the cavern and handed her the scissors. "I need you to cut my pants all the way up my leg, but I warn you, only my pants."

Alaina nodded again, trying to swallow the lump that was forming in her throat as she carefully cut the material covering his long muscular leg. She had never seen the naked flesh of a man, and she tried to stop her hand from shaking so fiercely.

When she finished, she dared not look up because she could feel that he was watching her carefully and she felt her cheeks burning. She thought she must be losing command of her mind, since she could not help thinking that his leg was somehow beautiful. It was long and strong, not unlike the powerful stallion he rode.

She felt his hand gently touch her chin and then lift her face to him. "I will take you to a safe place as soon as it's safe to do so, but for now, you'll just have to trust me."

She watched as he opened a bottle with the word vodka on it. It was forbidden for Muslims to drink alcohol and Alaina couldn't help staring as he took a drink of the forbidden liquid. Then, to her surprise, he poured it on his wound. She saw him straighten as if in great pain, but she didn't hear him utter a sound. He was large and looked brutal, yet her instinct told her that, at least for now, he was not going to hurt her.

She started to feel remorse at the pain she had caused this man, who quite possibly might have been trying to save her and had had kind words for her. Maybe she could trust him, and maybe he could take her to a safe place. She had not always lived in the desert; maybe there was a different place for her now.

The feeling of remorse went away as quickly as it had come when he handed her a needle and thread and expected her to sew the wound.

"Take off your veil so you can see," he said softly.

"It is forbidden." Strangely, now she felt almost defensive of her veil. All the times she had hated the thing, yet now she felt safer with it on, as if it could protect her from this man.

"You don't have to wear that thing around me."

No strange man should ask such a thing. But how could she help him if she couldn't see well, especially as dark as it was?

With one quick, easy motion, one she had perfected over the past years, she pulled off her veil.

Alaina blushed again as Alexander's gaze did not move from her face. He said with deliberation, "I'm glad to see the hatred in your cold blue eyes, Alaina; otherwise I'd think I've died and gone to Valhalla."

"You know of Valhalla?"

He smiled. "I will wind up there if you don't hurry with that needle. I'd do it myself, but I have a feeling you're a better seamstress than I am. Here, take a sip of this, it'll calm you."

Alaina looked at it. She started to shake her head, but as she saw his stern and unmoving gaze daring her to disobey him, she did as she was told. She felt a rush of water gather in her eyes as the liquid burned down her throat, but she also felt a wonderful warm sensation deep inside her as it ran into her empty stomach. She was shaking from cold and fear, and she decided to help herself to another swallow.

When she attempted a third sampling, Alexander pulled the bottle away from her. "That's enough, or I'll have to do the job myself," he muttered under his breath.

His words did not sound so kind this time and Alaina knew she couldn't let her guard down. Maybe if she was careful, he wouldn't kill her and would take her some place where she could again escape. She would have to trust him for now, but she would be careful also.

As if remorseful for startling her, Alexander's next words were said in a soothing tone, "Tell me what you were thinking about earlier, when you wept."

"I did not weep."

Alexander smiled, flashing perfect white teeth, and his features seemed to soften. Who was this man? He was not Arabic; for his eyes were lighter and different somehow, and they were wide set with well-arched brows above them. His chin was square and his nose straight and he had a look about him that said he didn't back down for anyone or anything. There was courage in the set of his jaw and the scar on his cheek that had paled with age showed he had been tested in this regard.

"All right, tell me what you were thinking that didn't make you cry. But tell me while you're stitching me up, before I bleed to death."

Alaina looked at his leg and saw he was losing a substantial amount of blood. She gained courage in that he had not punished her with extreme harshness for what she had done. She slowly began stitching, while he asked her again what she had been thinking about.

The alcohol loosened her tongue, and she told him about the time she was eight and the annual races were being held, with her grandfather running his prized mare. "I knew if the rider my grandfather had chosen were to ride in the race, he would not win. I was much lighter and a much better rider in my opinion than anyone in the village." She looked up wondering if he was angry with her boldness, but saw he was still smiling at her. She continued, "So I took it upon myself to help my grandfather win the race. I locked the rider in the house and dressed myself as a boy and entered the race. At the end of the race, I crossed over the finish line first and expected warm welcomes from all, but instead of the normal cheers and hugs and happy, smiling faces, everyone had walked away, leaving me to feel the shame of what I had done. It wasn't until later that I realized the embarrassment I had caused my family and friends by dressing as a man and breaking almost every rule of conduct that exists for a woman." Alaina finished sewing his wound.

There was neither anger nor rebuke in his next words, only kindness. "You're a very brave young woman, and I, for one, would have been proud of you for winning that race. But the ways of the West are different from those of this country, and you should understand that you are not of these people, that you have different longings inside you."

"I used to exasperate my mother to no end, but then she would hug me and call me her little western girl. It was almost as if she wished she could dare do the same things."

"Didn't she, when she was a girl?"

"My mother seldom spoke about the time she lived with her father. He only married one wife and they only had one child, my mother. They gave her everything that they would have given to a son. She was allowed to ride and have freedoms other women were not allowed in this country, and that was one of the reasons she was so sad, I think. It made being married to Ahmeed that much harder. He cares only for his sons while his wives and daughters are as chattel to him." Her sadness reached her voice.

"I know you are afraid of me, of what I might do to you, but I won't hurt you. Alaina, you don't belong here. You must have some family elsewhere I can take you to."

Could things really be so different elsewhere? Did she have family she could go to? But there was Devon Maxwell also. "My mother told me she has arranged my marriage to a man in America."

"Yes," he confirmed as he straightened his leg. He poured more vodka on his leg and took another strong drink out of the bottle.

"Do you know him?" she asked hopefully.

"I work for his company. He sent me to help you and your mother."

Alaina suddenly noticed the flag on the bottle and a strange pang entered her heart. "I know that flag! That's the Swedish flag! Svenska flaggan.

Sverige." She said the Swedish words in surprise. "I'd almost forgotten I speak that language. I wish I could remember more about my life before coming here to the desert. Maybe I do have family somewhere else." A ray of hope came flashing through her heart and she smiled.

Alexander returned the smile and said in a teasing tone, "I'll take you wherever you wish to go if you don't stab me anymore. But if you ever decide to stab someone else in the future, make sure you get him in a spot that will incapacitate him enough for you to escape, or you'll have to do this all over again."

Alaina could not help returning his smile, for it now seemed lazy and aloof somehow. She started feeling almost sheltered by his presence and allowed herself to relax slightly.

"Get some rest now," he said.

Having put some distance between them, she stretched out on the ground and tried to sleep, but her muscles instantly hurt as she tried to stretch them. They had been tense for too long.

"Come here," Alexander commanded softly. She obeyed because he had been kind to her, and she sat beside him. "Lean up against the wall behind you and mentally think about relaxing one muscle at a time." He watched her suffer from cramping in her legs for a few moments, and then swearing under his breath, pulled her roughly to him, landing her on his good leg.

Alaina immediately struggled against the intimate position. She was almost on this man's lap! She couldn't stay like this. "As long as you're cold, it will hurt," he said, trying to calm her. "Would you like to hear about the world beyond the desert?" he asked. "If you hold still, I will tell you about it."

She stopped struggling immediately. She could never learn enough about the world beyond this one. She nodded, trying to ignore how she was sitting. As he started to speak in his deep sonorous voice and she felt the warmth radiating from his chest, she was slowly able to relax.

"There is an island in the Pacific I visited some years ago that very few people know exists because it's still uncharted...." He started talking about tranquil seas and dolphins racing alongside large sailing vessels, about beautiful fish living in coral reefs and of majestic mountains towering over valleys of green pastures filled with wild flowers. She wanted to hear it all, but soon she couldn't keep awake. She drifted off thinking of beautiful flowers.

Her sleep was not restful though, and she awakened not long thereafter. She found it wasn't at all uncomfortable lying the way she was, but she noticed Alexander was still awake.

"Would you answer some questions for me?" He nodded. "Where do you live?" she asked softly, but not quietly enough to hide the apprehension she felt about asking a man such a personal question.

"Mostly in New York."

He didn't seem irritated with her for asking him a personal question, and she gained courage from that. "My mother, Zainab, always told me that one day I would travel to different places, where women are free to walk about without their faces covered, and women can do anything and everything they wish!"

"And would you like to do everything?" he asked, smiling at her.

"Well, yes, men can, why shouldn't I? I should like to travel to this place you spoke about earlier, and see many other places in the world—that's why my mother taught me Italian and had a tutor teach me Latin, French and English. But I think I know English the best."

Alexander looked at her in surprise, and then with interest, "I'm impressed."

Alaina smiled coyly, "I know you speak English because I've heard you use it."

Alexander laughed. "I guess you have. I'll confess if I had known you understood English, I would not have been as profane."

"I understand you were in pain when I stabbed you." She didn't know what else to say.

"This marriage to Devon Maxwell, do you agree with this arrangement?"

"I don't have much of a choice in these matters," she said slowly, but then her eyes adopted a dreamy quality about them. "But, I am happy with the match. I met him before when I was much younger and he is very tall and handsome, and very strong. He saved my life when I was a child. He is from a place called Wyoming, not New York."

"Sounds as if you're infatuated with a man you know nothing about." He had suddenly become more serious. "Maybe he is nothing like the man you imagine."

"My mother and her father like him. Grandfather Abdul is a wise man and if he likes this man, then there must be something good about him."

"Yes, Abdul is very wise."

"You know grandfather Abdul? Did he send you to rescue me from Mustafa?" She sat up and searched for confirmation to her question, longing for it to be true, but his eyes betrayed no answer.

"Yes, I met Abdul and he told me where Mustafa was headed. But I came because of a letter your mother had sent to Devon Maxwell. I would like to know how you feel about marrying someone you don't know or might not even like."

"But I told you I have met him, and I did like him. And besides, I have no one else." What she couldn't tell him was that all these years she had clung to the dreams of Devon Maxwell coming back for her, making her feel wanted and helping her cope with the feeling of being an outsider.

"Tell me about the time you met him," he said, sitting back and watching her. She hesitated and he prompted, "How old were you?"

"Around six."

"Quite young to make character judgments, don't you think?"

"Children often are more perceptive than adults about a person's true nature. Adults can often fool other adults, where they can't fool children."

"I stand corrected," he said grinning. Even his eyes seemed to smile—they were very blue right now. Alaina had never heard another man apologize before — and to her, a woman! She didn't care that it was for something unimportant; it still felt good. She realized she had been looking into his eyes far too long and she looked away embarrassed.

"Please, continue. Tell me more about your American."

"He saved me from a sinking ship." Why did he keep smiling at her? She really didn't remember much about him. "And he was nice to me," she added quickly.

"That's it?"

She thought he was mocking her now and she became angry. "He sent me a book after he'd returned to America." She didn't know why she felt she had to defend her liking for this man, but he just kept watching her, grinning, giving her strange feelings inside. "There's more," she continued.

"I'm all ears."

"He wrote a poem in my book. It was a book of fairy tales, and so was the poem." Her voice took on an ethereal quality as she continued, "It said:

Child of the pure, unclouded brow
And dreaming eyes of wonder!
Though time be fleet and I and thou
Are half a life asunder,
Thy loving smile will surely hail
The love-gift of a fairy tale."

Alexander still looked amused. "I hate to shatter your childhood fantasies, but the man you want to marry didn't write that, unless his name was Lewis Carroll."

"Who was he?"

"A man that died quite a while ago. And besides that small fact, I know Devon Maxwell, and he's not the poetic type."

"You know him well?"

"We're related. Is that all you remember?"

She decided to tell him everything now. "There was another man Devon saved also, and we floated to an island. I don't remember how long we were on the island before we were rescued, but I remember the man and Devon fighting, but not really fighting, more like a game. This other man wasn't like anyone I'd ever seen. Now that I'm older, I realize he must have been from Asia and that the game was him teaching Devon some kind of fighting techniques. They would give me food and at night I lay next to Devon by the fire to keep warm. That's all I remember. He took care of me and called me 'little princess'."

Now that he knew everything, she had to know some things. What if it was true that Devon Maxwell was not at all the man she dreamed him to be? What if he didn't want to marry her? Where would she go? "If you know this Devon, do you think he will want to take me as his wife?"

"Why would you think not?"

"He is from America, and in the West men and women marry out of love, not need, and besides, I have heard this man is very rich, and can buy anything he wants—just like grandfather Abdul can buy men with his oil."

Alexander seemed surprised by her perception and asked, "Did you see Abdul do this?"

"No, my grandfather would never let me see the foreigners that came to visit us, but I would sneak down the hallway to the balcony overlooking where they would sit and negotiate and listen as they spoke. I hope he is not like those men. In that case, I don't think I would be happy married to him."

"Yes, Devon is very rich. I'll take you to him if that's what you want, but first, we have to figure out a way to get you out of the country without Mustafa finding out our route."

"We could go to Jeddah, to my grandfather," she offered.

"No, Mustafa would look there first. I have another plan."

"But..."

"Sleep now while you can," he interrupted in his authoritative voice.

She wanted to get off his body, sensing his sudden change in mood, but he didn't allow her to get up. Not long after, she felt him drift off into sleep. She wondered at how quickly he could fall asleep, but then relaxed against him again, and fell asleep also.

His arm tightened around her as she fell back asleep and soon he could feel her breathing become deeper and more regular. He touched her long golden tresses that now hung down over her shoulder, curling alluringly right below her breasts. She was strikingly beautiful. Her features were perfect according to western standards, with magnificent almond shaped eyes that were intensely blue, retaining an innocence about them, yet a courage and inner strength he knew the desert life had imbued. Her beautifully arched eye brows and long lashes shaded a slender nose and delicate cheekbones leading to a sensuous mouth just asking to be kissed. Her rounded face and slightly pointed chin was stamped with her northern European ancestry.

He knew he should get some sleep, but he just held her for the next hour, feeling a powerful and strange longing to protect her, to take her away from this place. But he dared not voice these thoughts, nor act on them, for he had done so once in the past and it had nearly destroyed him.

It was time to go.

He lifted her gently from his lap and laid her carefully on the ground without waking her. He packed up his supplies and saddled Pegasus before he woke Alaina.

Alaina felt a nudge awaken her. "Its time to go. We must travel while it's still dark," he said.

Alaina opened her eyes slowly. She was lying on the hard ground, eye level with his boots. In the background she saw Pegasus saddled and ready to go. She groaned softly as she started to stand, but before she could straighten, she was lifted by strong arms and carried to Pegasus, and again found herself on top of this powerful beast.

"We must hurry, hold on!" he ordered, waking her out of her daze. She was not fast enough for his liking, "Now!"

She suddenly remembered why she disliked

him along with all men who were controlling, but then was thankful for his urging when again she felt the stallion's powerful muscles catapult them forward.

There was nothing for her to do except lean back into Alexander's chest and feel the rhythm and swaying of powerful strides beneath her. They rode for many hours.

She had no idea where she was when Alexander finally stopped and helped her off the stallion. They were standing in a valley of rock and stone with imposing walls of stone sculptured into columns all around them which formed a large entrance to a temple of some sort.

"Let's go," he urged as he let the stallion go and they started to walk.

"Where are we?" she asked wearily.

"A place Mustafa would never think of looking. It's an uncanny kind of place—not even Pegasus will enter here."

"Then I will not go in there either," she said shivering at the eeriness of the place.

"You do not have a choice. Either you walk or I drag you," he said firmly. He made good his threat as she hesitated, and lifted her into his arms again.

How had he cursed before? "You, you bastard! I wish your death by a vat of boiling oil! Let go of me, I will not go in there, animals know such things."

As they entered the ancient stone temple, he dropped her to her feet and explained as if to a small child, "You can sleep here for as long as you like; it's perfectly safe."

She shrugged and then rubbed her arms. She wondered if pagan rituals had taken place in these stone walls that were covered with strange drawings. She looked out toward the entrance and longed to run outside.

"And you will stay inside these walls," he ordered, as if reading her mind.

Alaina sat down, feeling emotionally drained from all that had happened. She shook from the cold and her own fear of this place and the anger she felt toward Alexander for making her stay here. She gathered her legs up against her breasts, holding them as she rocked herself slightly.

Alexander threw her a blanket and informed her, "I'm going to look for water."

"I don't care where you go," she replied.

As soon as he had left, she was sorry her anger had gotten the best of her. With Alexander gone she felt very much alone, and now the walls seemed to close in around her. She tried to think of her daydreams of old, of castles and princes, but it was as if the magic of it had vanished. She could not recapture her fantasies.

Alexander was gone for quite some time, but when he came back he carried a canteen of water with him. He offered the water to Alaina. As she drank, Alaina searched his expression, but found nothing she could interpret, except that he was ignoring her.

She watched him sit up against the wall, stretch his legs out in front of him, and close his eyes. She watched his face relax and found herself staring at him for some time. It was easy to see that he was not a man of leisure, but a man hard and trim from extensive physical activity. She had already seen his long legs and even though his *thobe*, the long shirt-like garment worn by Saudi men, covered his entire body, she knew more about him than any other man. He had not yet removed his *Ghutra*, which was the traditional headdress of Arab men, so she had not yet seen the hair on his head, but the hair on his legs had been very dark.

She finally turned around and lay down, wishing she could also find rest, but even more than that, feel comfortably safe in his arms again.

Several hours later she awakened to see Alexander saddling Pegasus outside. The temperature had already risen tremendously outside and she wondered why they were traveling during the daytime. "Where are we going?"

"You are staying here where it is safe. I'm riding back to your grandfather to make sure Mustafa isn't holding any hostages and waiting for us," Alexander said, mounting up.

"You'll be all alone against many. They might kill you!"

"Worried for my well being, my dear? I'm flattered, but wasn't it only a few hours ago you hated me and wished my death in boiling oil?" His eyebrows arched up and he made an obvious attempt to suppress a grin.

"Oh, I do," she said angrily, not wanting to be left behind, "but if you die, then no one will know where I am."

"Ah, the true reason for your concern, and a selfish one at that. Anything I can bring you?" he asked, still grinning. But he did not wait for her answer.

Alaina tried to remember every profanity she had heard from him; she did not know what they meant, but yelled them at him anyway. Alaina could hear him laughing loudly as he rode off.

# Chapter 4

It was the longest wait of Alaina's life. She paced for many hours wondering if this man, who was a mystery to her, would come back for her, or if she was doomed to die here. Would Mustafa eventually find her here? If he did, what kind of life would she lead? Would she be trapped in a village with many children around her making no use of the education she had received from her mother? What was the alternative? There was Devon Maxwell. He had been a part of her life, in her dreams since she was six years old. Her mother wanted her to marry him, and only two days ago she had been thrilled by the prospect of it coming true, but now ....

There was Alexander. He was strong and could defend her, and she admittedly found him very attractive, more so than any man she had seen in her isolated life. More so than the English doctors she had seen in the hospital. There was something about his eyes, something concealed, and something deep inside she wanted to know about. It was as if there were walls built around the man, and it was disconcerting. She never knew exactly what he was thinking or feeling. But when he smiled at her, she would feel something strange she couldn't understand and an unfamiliar tugging at her heart.

Yet she had to fulfill her mother's dying wish to marry Devon Maxwell, if he wanted her.

Life was becoming more confusing at every turn.

She finally decided she would wait a few more hours and then, if Alexander did not return, she would set out on her own to find her grandfather. He would know what to do, and she couldn't believe he would make her marry Mustafa. If Devon Maxwell would not marry her, maybe grandfather Abdul would send her to Italy or France where she could live her life in quiet, even if it meant being alone. She had been alone most of her life anyway, only the love from her mother had kept her from complete isolation.

Her mother. She'd had a different mother once, one she couldn't remember very well, but now that she had lost a mother a second time, all the pain and tears burst forward, intensified. She was alone now, without any distractions from her emotions, and she couldn't stop the tears any longer. She sat against the stone wall, her arms hugging her legs to her chest, crying long and deep until she was so exhausted sleep overcame her.

She awakened at the sound of footsteps. Alexander had come back.

"I brought you a few things," he said softly, as he handed her a large canvas bag. She realized he'd noticed she'd been crying by the way he looked sympathetically at her now.

"Zainab's mother packed this bag for you along with some papers and bank accounts I have in Pegasus' saddle bag. Zainab kept them with her mother and father for safety. They now belong to you."

"Did they say anything else?"

"They wish you happiness and agree I should help you leave the country. They know Mustafa will come looking for you. I think we should leave as soon as possible, after we have eaten and when you're ready."

"I have not grown fond of this place," she answered.

He smiled and escorted her out. She saw he had another horse with him and recognized the mare almost instantly. "This was my grandfather's favorite filly the last time I was there. How did you get her?" She approached the mare and patted her gleaming neck.

"It's a gift for you."

She looked in disbelief. She searched Alexander's face for the truth, but his blank expression told her nothing. "My grandfather would never have given such a gift to me, a woman."

"He cares for you."

"Then maybe I could go and live with them," she said expressing the feeling of hope that entered her.

"Mustafa would come after you. Unless that is the life you want, we need to get you out of this country. Mustafa's father and your grandfather are old enemies. He meant to take out revenge on you for things that happened long ago."

She had never heard anyone mention Mustafa before a day ago. Had it only been a day? "What happened between grandfather Abdul and Mustafa?"

"Many years ago, Abdul's father went to the United States with some horses to sell and there he met Devon Maxwell's grandfather. They became friends and over the years those two men continued to breed their horses. Maxwell's thoroughbreds are now heavily influenced by Arabian blood, and Abdul's Arabians are mixed with thoroughbred blood."

"That's why grandfather's horses are the fastest in the desert!" Alaina said.

"Yes, but Abdul's father, and later Abdul, had business dealings with Maxwell's grandfather. Later, when oil flowed richly from Arabian ground, both families gained from joint business ventures. In the beginning, Devon Maxwell's grandfather invested more money, because of the gold his father had mined during the gold rush, later, Abdul had more money to invest.

"Many years ago Mustafa's father became interested in one of Abdul's horses. A colt bred for speed and unlike any other. That horse was Pegasus." He patted his horse lovingly. "He was born and raised here in the desert. Mustafa's father captured Pegasus, but while doing so, Pegasus killed his oldest son."

"So Mustafa and Abdul are enemies?"

Alexander nodded.

Alaina continued, beginning to understand, "And what started out as a mutual interest in breeding horses became business ventures that made both families wealthy. So is my marriage to Devon Maxwell to cement the bond between the two families to a greater degree?"

Alexander didn't answer her directly. "It would seem a way to keep you safe from Mustafa. But you have another home," Alexander answered softly, pulling out papers from the saddlebag. "It seems Zainab had made inquiries, secretly through her father, regarding your native family."

"You mean I have blood relatives somewhere?"

"You have, at least as of this writing dated a few years ago."

"I don't understand, why didn't anyone tell me?"

"I wish I knew the answer, but we might be able to figure out something from this correspondence."

At first the words didn't make any sense to her. She studied the foreign words, trying to apply the different languages she did speak, but it didn't work. Not until she relaxed her mind and didn't try quite so hard did she start to understand. Alaina looked over the correspondence, carefully holding the letters that were a link to a past she did not know but that could now alter her future. "It says I have an uncle and cousins in Germany." She looked at Alexander. "But why wasn't I told earlier? Why didn't they tell me or send me to them?"

"Weren't you happy growing up here?"

Alaina didn't answer. She would not tell him of her loneliness and of her longings to be like the other children and people of the village, and how she had suffered for her different skin and hair color, and eye color that gave her away even if everything else could be covered.

"Rough childhood?" he asked.

He had asked with such bitterness in his voice that Alaina swallowed her tears and looked into his blue eyes. For a moment she thought she saw pain. She hesitantly put her hand up to his cheek, and, filled with compassion, started to say, "I'm sorry..." But she stopped and pulled her hand away as she saw an intensity in his eyes that had not been there before. Her lips parted slightly in surprise as she felt him pull her into his arms. She suddenly felt weak and slightly afraid as her heart pounded quickly against her ribs and she felt she couldn't swallow.

Alaina had never been kissed before and at first she wasn't sure she liked it, but then, as his tongue touched her lips, coaxing, delicately exploring, almost tormentingly gentle, she forgot her fear and started imitating his actions, kissing him back. Her arms came around his neck and that's when his kiss changed from gentle to demanding, devouring, stealing her breath away, and making her head feel drugged. Alaina felt lost in a stream of emotions, her body reacting without her permission. She felt herself answering his kisses and molding her body into his. His kisses trailed down her neck toward her breast, and she felt her head swirling.

What was he doing to her? It must stop. She didn't want him to stop. She didn't know what she should do and before she could stop herself, she whispered, "Please!"

Alexander stopped instantly. He had seen the limitless empathy in her eyes and that had been his undoing. Here this young woman had lost everything in one day and yet was reaching out to him, to comfort him—a purely unselfish act. He wanted to kiss her inviting lips, to crush her body to his and take away the pain he knew she was feeling, a pain he understood all too well.

Just a kiss.

He looked at her beautiful face and her eyes that now opened slowly, questioningly. There had been much more to that one kiss than he had intended, and he needed to turn the situation around quickly if he was going to drop her off in Germany.

She was young and innocent, too much so, for his liking.

He smiled at her dazed eyes. "Ah, Alaina, you are so lovely, but you are so young." He carefully straightened her thin gown which revealed so much, too much, of her youthful body, and then a mocking smile twisted his handsome mouth as he said with deliberate superiority, "It's best you dress yourself more modestly if you wish to remain the innocent little girl that you are."

Alaina's mind cleared quicker than her body could recover. Her heart was still pounding and the feeling of warmth that had spread through her body was still lingering, but his words screamed through her mind and jolted into her consciousness. "Little girl!" Alaina repeated. "Little girl!" She could not contain her anger. "Why, you, cad... you oaf... you monkey and any other bad English word I don't know. I wish you would just fall off your horse and hit your conceited, thick head."

How dare he catch her off guard, make her feel wild wonderful things that attacked all her senses, and then discard her as if it had never happened!

She grabbed at the bag of clothes he had brought for her and felt angry at herself for feeling comfortable enough around this man not to dress immediately in more suitable attire upon his return. She pulled out an emerald green suit and turned her back to Alexander, who had the decency to leave. She dressed hastily. She decided to stay away from Alexander, who she could see was now building a fire outside.

As an hour went by, she was having serious doubts whether she would ever feel calm again; she still felt the warmth of Alexander's body on hers, and where he had kissed her, her flesh still burned.

Alexander walked in, bringing food with him. She turned her back to him, showing him that he had hurt her pride. He put his hand on her shoulder and wouldn't let her pull away. "Alaina," he said softly, but then more firmly when she wouldn't answer. "Eat now. We ride at sunset."

He was back to his normal authoritative voice and Alaina understood more and more that he was a man used to giving orders and being obeyed, and that the gentleness he showed her was not his normal manner.

"We must ride swiftly and get to the harbor while it's still dark so I can smuggle you aboard a ship. I'm sure Mustafa has his men everywhere looking for a man and a woman and a black horse. I suspect his main concern will be the airport, which is why we are staying clear of it. And now it's time we practice your English, my dear. From now on we shall speak only English. Now, quickly go and change into these clothes." He threw her some clothes he had taken out of her bag.

She saw they were jeans and a T-shirt. "I can't wear men's clothing!" she gasped.

He smiled at her sense of propriety. "You'd be surprised at what girls your age wear in America." Then, on a more somber note, he added, "Wear them."

She didn't understand why he wanted her to change again, especially into pants. She had never worn pants before and they felt uncomfortable on her legs, rubbing her soft skin.

He smiled at the confused look on her face as she came back dressed in the jeans he had received from Zainab's mother. His first reaction was that of humor, but as he looked her over, he saw what Alaina had seen, that her grandmother's jeans were just a little tight on her, showing off her full figure, and the blouse exposed more than it should. He sighed. "I was hoping there'd be a chance at passing you off as a man, but I can see now that idea is futile. Wear your Abaaya over the clothes until we get to the harbor."

Alaina put on the long, black cloak that was worn by all Saudi women over their clothing and then mounted the mare with graceful ease. She was happy to be riding her own horse, not having to sit in front of the man that so easily could rob her body of its own will. She was determined she wouldn't allow that to happen again.

# Chapter 5

They rode speedily through the desert sands, Alexander apparently knowing exactly where he was going, arriving many hours later at a harbor, where people were just starting to move around in the early morning hours. Alexander found a Greek vessel that was departing the next day on route to Italy. He made arrangements with the captain directly, paying him sufficiently to make sure he kept his mouth shut and ensuring they could board immediately. They took care of their horses, making sure they had decent stalls and feed, and then Alexander escorted her to their cabin. Alexander saw eyes watching the beautiful Alaina as her blond hair whipped out from underneath her hood by the force of the wind. Alexander protectively put his arm around her as he escorted her, but Alaina was not inclined to appreciate his attentiveness after his last show of affection.

He held her tighter and whispered threateningly in her ear, "Move away and I'll have to embrace and kiss you right here. To everyone on this ship, you are my wife, and you will act accordingly while eyes are watching." She was about to protest when he added, "Unless you'd prefer to share quarters with someone else on this ship, quarters not as comfortable and with someone with less honorable intentions, I suggest you smile lovingly at me now and nod."

Alaina smiled up at him, doing as she was told, but asked scornfully, "And are you honorable?"

"My dearest, I am as honorable as they come. It's my intentions you should be questioning." His smile was dazzling and teasing, but his quiet, deep voice seemed serious enough. She nodded her acknowledgment and gave him a quick kiss on the cheek before they entered the small cabin they were to occupy on their journey.

She looked around at the desk and chair in one corner, a chest, and a small bed on the opposite wall. "Where are we to sleep?" she asked.

He sat down on the bed and patted it for her to join him. He saw her staring at him in disbelief and he sighed. "After days and nights in the desert alone together, I have ruffled nothing more than a feather or two, I fight for your life, save you from the evil clutches of Mustafa, get stabbed...."

"Stop, please," she said looking around. "I'll sleep on the floor."

"Women!" Alexander muttered as he walked out the door and locked it behind him.

Alaina didn't know what she had done to anger him, but was thankful for the time she had alone. She poured some water into the basin and washed her face and hands, and then lay down on the bed to rest for a few minutes.

Alexander went to have a talk with the captain who wanted to discuss Alaina.

"Your wife...she is truly beautiful, no?" he said in a heavy Greek accent.

"Yes, and I would like to keep her safe. Are there any other keys to our cabin?"

"No, Monsieur Alexander, you have the only

one," he said, smiling at Alexander, his eyes glistening. The man was nearly as tall as Alexander, somewhere in his early forties, and Alexander didn't trust him.

"I am in need of a few things before we depart. Can I pay one of your men to buy them and deliver them to me? I will pay you too, of course, for his services." Alexander did not want to leave Alaina alone anywhere on this ship. He pulled out some money, letting the Greek see the large knife that he kept in his belt, and then placed it into the Greek's outstretched hand.

"Of course, money always talks, especially American dollars." The captain called one of his stewards, and, in a language Alexander did not understand, gave orders.

Alexander returned to the cabin and silently opened the door. He found Alaina peacefully sleeping, stretched out on the bed. He sat in the only chair in the room, stretched his long legs out in front of him, favoring his injured one slightly as he crossed them at the ankles, and drifted into a light sleep.

As Alaina woke from her sleep, she saw Alexander and watched him for a minute, stretching her aching muscles. He had taken off his head covering and she could see his hair was a dark rich brown. He was quite handsome. If only he wouldn't make her so angry all the time and be so bossy, she'd like him a lot better.

Fresh air, she decided, was what she needed, and when she couldn't open the small window in the room, she very quietly, so as not to wake Alexander, started for the door.

Alexander opened one eye and watched her patiently. "Do not go out that door alone, ever," he said softly, yet very firmly.

"I just want some fresh air," she responded.

"Never alone, do you understand?" He waited for her to acknowledge his command. "If you want to go out on deck, or anywhere else on this ship, you go only with me." She wanted to protest, but he added bluntly, "Even the dear captain of this fine vessel wants you to warm his bed. You are in a world no longer protected by the walls of your home or village. And there is still the threat of Mustafa finding you. You must trust me."

She nodded and obediently sat back down on the bed, wondering how long she'd have to wait.

"I'm waiting for someone," he said with his eyes still closed. A few minutes later a knock sounded on their cabin door. He got up and opened the door to allow the shipmate to enter. He received a large bag of supplies and a smaller box that he opened immediately. He took out a small pistol and, looking at the man who had delivered the items, pointed to the housing and asked, "Where is the ammunition?"

The steward pulled his eyes away from Alaina and smiled at Alexander as if they shared some secret. He reached into his pockets and pulled out a large bag of bullets. Alexander filled the pistol while keeping his eyes on the little man who couldn't seem to take his eyes of Alaina. He stepped up to the man, getting his full attention now, and with eyes that radiated Arctic cold, he told the man, "You tell the other men on this ship that I know how to use this and I will if anyone crosses me."

The smaller man backed away as he nodded, the smile erased from his face. He left the room with great urgency.

Alaina watched as he carefully checked the gun to make sure it was clean and working properly. She knew by the way he handled it that he had used one many times before.

Alexander handed the gun to her, "Just in case, I think you should know how to use this."

"Just in case, what?" she asked.

"Try not to worry too much. I will see you safely to your new home, or wherever your heart desires."

"And then?" she asked softly.

'And then, my dear, I will go back to my busy, but peaceful life, before you entered it." He avoided her eyes, instead moving behind her to show her how to aim and fire.

"I don't like this thing," she said giving it back.

"Well then, let's hope you never have to use it," he said tucking it away. "Come, let's get some fresh air."

As he escorted her out the door, Alaina instantly noticed a difference in him. His body became slightly tense, and it seemed his senses were heightened, almost like an animal, ready to attack any unsuspecting prey. It made her feel uneasy.

"I think we should go inside again," he said. Before Alaina could protest, he added, "I have long ago learned to trust my instincts." Then he said in a lighter tone, "Besides, I think I should like a bath. How about you?"

Alaina immediately became indignant at his suggestion and he laughed, "I didn't mean the two of us together, although if that's what you have in mind...." They entered the cabin and she hit him in the stomach with a well-placed elbow. He just laughed harder at her and leaving the cabin again, said, "Wait here, I'll have some men bring a tub and water."

Soon, Alexander returned with a large metal tub and two men who were hauling water for him. She smiled in delight as the tub was filled with fresh steaming water and Alexander, bowing gracefully, said, "For you, my lady."

Alaina was so grateful and excited about finally having a bath again she began taking off her clothes without a thought of Alexander standing in the room watching her. Suddenly she realized her mistake and looked pleadingly at him, "Please..."

"Yes, yes, I'm leaving. I'll be nearby if you need me. Oh, by the way, I had this perfumed soap bought earlier for your first bath. Don't drown."

She quickly undressed and sank down in the warm water, completely submerging herself in the tub. She added the perfumed soap, swishing it around in the water until it made mounds of soft bubbles all around her, wondering at how thoughtful Alexander had been. Certainly, it was a luxury to bathe on a ship, and he had afforded it for her. *He could be so nice when he wanted to be,* she thought, and her mind drifted back to his kiss. It had not at all been distasteful. She remembered the slightly salty taste on his lips, and the way he smelled of leather and horses. She pictured him riding on his horse with great ease and command and could picture him as a knight coming to save her.

She was still-half dreaming as she looked up from the water and saw a dark face in the porthole. She screamed and Alexander was instantly in their cabin. She lamely pointed to the porthole, which now was empty, and felt embarrassed to the tips of her toes that she had screamed. If only she hadn't been dreaming she would have thought better of it.

"So we have a Peeping Tom," he said going to the porthole and covering it with a towel. Then he turned around and faced her, taking in her expression. His voice took on a teasing tone again, and one eyebrow lifted slightly, "Excuse the intrusion, wife, but I came at your somewhat urgent call for help."

Alaina sank deeper down into the tub, but not before she realized he had found pleasure in the sight he beheld. "Need your back scrubbed?" he asked coming closer.

"Stay away!" she warned, splashing him with water, and adding threateningly, "Or I'll scream again!"

"My sweet," he continued, his eyes mocking her, "you are my wife, no one would dare enter here, not while I'm in here." He watched her eyes narrow as she flashed them angrily at him. He smiled then and added dryly, "Some day, you might ask a man to take a bath with you, but since that won't be today, kindly lower yourself back into the water to keep yourself modestly covered up."

Mortified by her immodesty, which had been caused only by the anger he had made her feel, she sank deep into the water, her face turning many shades of red before she calmed herself.

Alexander sat down in the chair, stretching his legs out in front of him, to further observe his trustee. What a delightful young woman she was turning out to be; he had not laughed so much in years. The steam rose from the hot water and flushed her checks, while the ends of her long hair swirled about her breasts as if they were alive in the water.

"I'm glad you're enjoying yourself," she said irritated over his boldness.

"Let me join you and my joy will be complete," he said, smiling broadly as his eyes took on a devilish look.

"If you don't have the decency to leave this room, then at least turn around and give me the privacy to dress. I want to get out." Alaina caught a look on his face that said she had ruined some of his fun, but he turned around, went to his bag, pulled out a large shirt, and threw it to her.

"It might not be your size, but it's clean."

Alaina pulled it on and sure enough, it went down to her knees. She quickly buttoned the shirt, sensing that she was taking too much time and that soon he would turn around.

When he did face her, he smiled sincerely and complimented her, "It even looks good on you." He went to her and rolled up the sleeves. "We'll dine in tonight. The captain understands we are fatigued. Contingent on his keeping our passage secret, I bribed him with enough money that he's probably off making plans how to spend it all."

A knock sounded at the door and a man brought two more buckets of hot water to add to the bath. Alexander immediately started unbuttoning his pants and he laughed softly as Alaina quickly turned around.

As she heard him lower into the bath water, Alaina didn't know what to do with herself in the small room without facing him. What would her mother say if she could see her now?

"Alaina, come scrub my back."

Without facing him, she could not be sure if he was serious. She reasoned with herself that he was probably submersed sufficiently in the water and that she really wouldn't see much, especially if she kept her eyes on his face. Finally she sat on the bed and faced him. She couldn't help giggling when she saw how uncomfortable he looked with his knees sticking up out of the water and his chest still completely dry. "Maybe you should have gotten a bigger tub," she teased.

He scowled at her, "Unfortunately, this room couldn't hold a bigger one." He held out the scrub brush to her. She hesitated, but then obeyed him as she was getting used to doing. But she noticed he only grew more uncomfortable with her standing so close. "Harder," he growled. She bent into her work more and he suddenly took the brush away from her hand and mumbled something under his breath.

Alaina smiled to herself, but jumped back as he suddenly started getting out. She turned to face the little porthole again and she saw through the towel that it was getting dark outside. She waited as she heard him dressing.

Alexander put on clean pants and took a razor out of his bag. He had acquired a rather lengthy growth in the last few days, and she could tell it was not familiar to him, that it seemed almost uncomfortable for him.

Alaina watched in fascination for never had she seen anyone shave their face before. Alaina couldn't imagine what he would look like without the dark brown beard covering his face.

Eventually he turned around, and Alaina found herself starring at him in surprise, for he was even more handsome than she could have ever imagined. The beard did not hide a weak chin or thick lips, his face was ruggedly beautiful, his chin strong and square and his lips almost sensual as he smiled at her now.

Alaina, realizing that she was staring, turned red from her toes to her ears. She looked away.

He seemed pleased with her response and reached for her chin, turning her face towards his, and said, "It's all right, I must look quite different to you without a beard."

She nodded, sensing that he was trying to minimize the embarrassment she felt and smiled appreciatively at him.

They enjoyed a rather quiet and peaceful dinner together. Alexander didn't tease her and she relaxed to the wine and conversation, which now centered on her mare. “Can we go see them later?”

“Sure,” he said getting up, “let's go now.” She nodded. She took his hand as they walked out. As they walked along the deck, she thought to herself that now they really did look like a couple.

She was happy to see Lady, and the horses neighed excitedly at their approach. They saw that they had plenty of clean water and food.

“The captain is caring for our horses as if they were his own!” said Alaina, wondering how much Alexander had paid him.

“We must give them a good cleaning tomorrow.”

Alaina looked happily up at Alexander. “Thank you so much for bringing her to me, and taking her along on the trip to my new life. Now I'll have something to take along with me from the past into the future. Some day I'll repay you for everything, I promise.”

“We'll see,” he said abruptly. They strolled the length of the ship and Alaina was fascinated that so much steel and wood could float on the sea. “Where are we going?”

“We'll be traveling through the Suez Canal and then up through the Mediterranean to a port near Rome."

She had always been good at geography and knew Germany was still a distance from Rome. “Have you ever been to Germany?” she asked now turning toward him.

He continued looking out over the water. “Yes, a few years ago. It's a beautiful country.” He looked at her for a moment, not saying anything, and then started walking back to their cabin. “Let's go get some sleep.”

Alaina noticed that he limped slightly and wondered if the soap in the water had irritated his wound. As they got to the cabin door, Alexander told her, "Kiss me like a good little wife, for all the people to see." She gave him a peck on the check. He laughed, "I guess that's what I get when I ask you for a good wife's kiss." He then kissed her forehead and unlocked the door.

He untied what had looked like a web and quickly turned out to be a hammock. "This is my bed, and that is yours," he said pointing to the bed in the room. "Please do not argue with me," he said as she was about to protest, "you will find that you will lose."

His annoyed tone warned her not to persist. She removed her pants and quickly got into bed. Alaina thought about her horse and the land called Germany as she fell asleep

Alexander sighed as he watched her. He checked the pistol, then swung himself into the hammock and closed his eyes.

Sometime during the night he was awakened by whispering. He squinted one eye slightly open and found two men entering the room, one heading for Alaina, the other for his hammock. He clicked the pistol into firing position and watched as the men froze. "Get out slowly," he snarled, "and keep your hands where I can see them."

Alaina, waking at Alexander's voice, sat up clutching the sheets to her. Alexander jumped out of the hammock in one fluid movement while keeping the gun pointed at the two men. "Out the door slowly," he commanded, following them out and signaling Alaina to move close to his back for protection.

"Now over to the railing, mates." As the men obeyed, he said in a menacing tone, "So you thought you'd steal my wife from me now, did you? Well, what's mine is mine and I intend to keep what's mine." His deep voice carried throughout the ship to any listening ears. "Now climb over the railing, before I shoot your balls off." If they did not understand his language, they certainly understood his meaning as he took aim at one of the men's pants. They quickly jumped into the water below.

Alaina sagged against him slightly, frightened to think that some other man might have taken her again. Alexander put his arm around her and they walked very slowly back to the cabin. Alaina could feel him straining and looked down at his leg. She gasped and stopped a moment.

"Do not say a word, and do not act as if anything is wrong. Just keep moving back to the cabin."

She understood that he did not want anyone on board to know that he was injured. Alaina said nothing until they got back to the cabin behind locked doors.

Alaina stared at the blood-soaked material of his pants. "Why didn't you tell me?" she asked.

"It must have gotten worse while I was asleep," he said, undoing his pants. For once, prudence left Alaina and she helped him.

With his pants at his ankles, she pushed him down onto the bed and made him lie down. "I am going to treat this wound, and you will sleep here tonight. I will sleep in the hammock. And do not argue with me, for you will lose," she said mimicking him.

"Is that how I sound?" he asked, frowning.

"Worse," she said, as she got his first aid kit out. "We have to get some boiling water."

"Alaina..." he started to protest, when she opened the door and stuck her head out to see if anyone was about. Someone came walking by a few moments later and she signaled to him to come closer. She showed him a handful of coins and asked for hot water. The man came back promptly with steaming hot water in two large buckets.

"You learn quickly," Alexander mumbled, sleep overcoming him.

Alaina watched him fall asleep as she tore some cloths from the bed sheet and dipped them into the hot water. Ignoring the pain to her hands as the water scalded them, she folded the cloths together into a compress and gently placed it on his leg.

Alexander jumped up out of the bed, throwing the rag from him. He saw she was trying to clean the wound. "Warn me next time, will you?"

"You were sleeping. I hoped you'd sleep through it all."

He frowned at her, but allowed her to clean his wound.

She then put a salve from his first aid kit on it, ripped some more sheets, and bandaged the wound. "Now sleep."

His eyes were already closed. Alaina understood the many sleepless nights were taking their toll, and his body was no longer capable of fighting off the infection that now traveled through it.

Alaina watched as his body relaxed and hoped he would sleep for a long while. Now feeling somewhat less secure, she went back to the door to be certain it was locked. She looked at Alexander, his face now relaxed and looking much younger, his strong body now less overwhelming, and a feeling of softness came into her heart for this man who continually saved her.

She took it upon herself to protect and take care of Alexander, although looking at him again, even asleep, hc hardly seemed helpless. She sighed and picked up the gun, trying to remember how to hold it. After some time of swinging around and aiming at the door knob, she felt better, thinking she could fire and actually hit something.

Alexander started tossing on the small bed and Alaina knew it was a fever. She took a towel, dipped it in the water that had cooled down, and put it on his forehead. His tossing was becoming more violent, and she had to hold the cloth in place.

A knock sounded on the door. What was she going to do? She knew no one must find out that Alexander was sick. She heard him moaning and shout out, and winced as the knock came again. An idea came to her, and hoping she was doing the right thing, she ripped her blouse from the neck down. She had seen in the mirror that her left eye had a dark black circle under it, from Mustafa's fist, and now with her hand holding her blouse closed, she hoped as she opened the door slightly, anyone would jump to the right conclusion.

A young man, no more than fourteen or fifteen, stood in front of her door with the morning sunrise peering over his shoulder. He hastily delivered his message. "The captain wants you to join him for lunch," he said in a strange English dialect.

"Tell the captain that my husband is not in the mood and that I would be most appreciative if we could take our meals in our cabin."

The boy heard a moan and tried to look in the room, but Alaina closed the door somewhat and hoped he had not seen anything. She added, "He's been drinking, and doesn't want to see anyone."

The boy, hearing the distress in her voice and obviously misinterpreting the reason, asked softly, "Are you all right?"

She nodded and smiled sweetly at the young

man, "Thank you for asking, though. Could you do me a favor? I'll pay you." She didn't wait for him to answer. "Whenever you can, could you bring me some fresh water, but don't let anyone know. Do you promise? If you tell, I would be very unhappy, but if you keep your favor to me a secret, I'll reward you greatly when we land." He nodded and Alaina closed the door, hoping he would be discreet.

Alexander had thrown off the covers and his shirt was drenched in sweat. She unbuttoned the shirt and hesitated a moment as she saw the expanse of his powerful upper body, from his muscular chest and wide shoulders that were broad enough to cover the entire bed, to his flat, hardened stomach where the sheet still clung to him. He moaned again and she instantly felt guilty for just staring at him instead of doing something for him. She couldn't roll him over to get the shirt off his body, so she left it on his back and soaked the towel in the cool water to wash off his face and chest. She continued faithfully to wash him off with the cool water, sometimes just brushing her hand over his forehead and through his thick hair, while talking softly to him.

She was so intent on what she was doing that she jumped when she heard a knock on the door again. She hoped it was the young man and not the captain or another shipmate. She opened the door slowly and relief flooded through her when she saw it was the young man.

"I brought you your lunch. I'll bring water as soon as I can. How is he feeling?"

Surprised at his perceptive observation, Alaina asked, "How...?"

"It's okay," he interrupted. "You can trust me; I won't tell a soul. I know why you're afraid to let anyone know. I told the captain that your husband told me that you weren't feeling well and that you needed rest."

"Why would you do that for me?"

The young man shrugged his shoulders. Alaina wanted to hug him, but instead she signaled him in, feeling now she could trust him with the whole truth. And besides, she was now becoming anxious that Alexander was still asleep and had not awoken. She had cleaned out his wound again. It was still festering, and she knew she should be doing something else for him, but she didn't know what.

The young man took one look at Alexander and then his leg, and spoke softly to Alaina. "He is very sick, no? He needs medicine or else he will lose the leg. I have seen it happen before to a man on this ship. They had to take his leg. Later he killed himself, not wanting to live as a cripple."

Alaina winced at his words. She starting thinking of Alexander with just one leg and a lump formed in her throat. She knew she had to do whatever it took to prevent that.

"What medicine? How do I get it?"

"I will get it for you when the doctor is asleep tonight."

"I can't let you do that. I'll do it myself."

"No, please, you must not do that. They will know you are unprotected. I have seen what these men do to women, and I don't want you to suffer their fate."

"May I know your name?" she asked.

"Ian."

Alaina looked into his gray eyes and asked, "That's an English name, isn't it?"

Ian shrugged. "I don't know where I'm from. They tell me I was found alone at a harbor as a small boy. The captain here took pity on me and brought me with him on his travels."

"I'm sorry," she whispered with understanding. "You know, we're very much alike. I lost my family when I was very young and other people raised me. Now they are dead and I don't know where the future will take me."

"What about your husband, hasn't he given you a home?"

"Oh yes, well, we just got married and I'm on my way to my new home." Alaina had never lied before and she hoped she wouldn't give herself away.

Ian nodded, seeming satisfied with the answer and said, "I need to go, but I'll be back tonight. I'll knock twice and then twice again, so you will know it's me."

"Be careful."

"I always am," Ian replied grinning, and then left silently.

# Chapter 6

As Alexander slept, Alaina thought back to the words he had spoken earlier on the deck to the two men. He had called her *his*. He had said that he intended on keeping what was his. She knew it was only part of their disguise, but she couldn't help thinking how wonderful those words sounded. She had always wanted to belong.

Suddenly he sat up. "You tramp!" he shouted. "Michelle, we're through and you...." Alexander fell back and murmured words Alaina couldn't understand.

"Alexander?" she asked softly. "Are you awake?"

He grabbed her arm roughly, "Leave me alone, I told you, we're through. You're worse than a bitch in...." He let go of her arm as quickly as he'd grabbed it.

Alaina rubbed her arm and felt grateful she was not the true recipient of his animosity. "It's me, Alaina," she said. Who was Michelle?

"I was foolish enough to love you once, but...." Then his voice faded. Alaina saw the anguish etched into his features at that moment, and heard the pain in his bitter words. She wanted to hold him, to take the suffering away, but the fear of being mistaken for this Michelle stopped her. Who was this person that could hurt him so much that it haunted his dreams? Was it someone in his past or present? How little she knew of this man.

During the next few hours, Alexander mumbled more in his sleep, adding bits and pieces to the picture Alaina had formed of his life, but Alaina had trouble understanding most of it. Anger about his father and about betrayal. He whispered words of torment and turned to lie on his stomach as if to stop the pain. And then he was silent.

Too silent.

Alaina saw her chance to remove the soiled shirt from his back now, and she gently removed it.

She gasped. Horrible scars covered his back. They went in every direction and she wondered what could have caused them. She gently glided her fingers over these old wounds as a lump filled in her throat and tears burned her eyes. "What have they done to you? How many people have hurt you?" she whispered hoarsely.

Two consecutive sets of knocks sounded on the cabin door and as Alaina opened it, Ian smiled brightly and held up two bottles of what looked like medicine. "The old doc didn't hear a thing," he boasted.

"He seems to be in terrible pain and now he's rolled over on his wound," Alaina told Ian.

Ian went to see if he could help turn him over, but stopped short at the sight of his back. "Holy..." he stopped himself and looked at Alaina, "Sorry, I'm not used to being around a lady."

"What do you think happened?" Alaina asked.

"Hard to tell," Ian answered examining the damage. "I'd say either he was in the wrong place at the wrong time, or someone really hated him. Come on, help me turn him. He sure is heavy."

The two turned Alexander over so that they could administer the medicine. Ian held Alexander's head up at an angle so that Alaina could pour a little of the medicine down his throat. "I hope this helps," Ian said.

"Oh, Ian, it has to help," Alaina said. "It's all my fault—I did this to him—I stabbed him."

"You did this? I bet that hurt."

"I didn't mean to..." tears welled up in her eyes.

"No, I meant his pride," Ian said. "I think it will be all right, really. He's strong and by the looks of him, I'd say extremely healthy. He survived that whipping, and that must have been a lot worse than this, believe me."

"I hope you're right."

"I'll return the salve, but you keep the medicine and give it to him every four hours or so. That's what I've heard the doctor say before, anyway." He got up and headed for the door.

Alaina went to him. "Ian, how can I ever thank you?"

Ian smiled and shrugged.

"Please try to think of a way."

He nodded and added, "I'll bring you some food, and some broth for your husband as soon as I can." And then he was gone.

Alaina continued to sit by Alexander's side, feeling her head become heavier and heavier, but determined not to fall asleep in case Alexander needed her.

Alexander awakened and found her sitting on the edge of the bed next to him with her chin resting on her chest and sound asleep. He grinned as he realized she had been sitting at his side for quite some time. He took some strands of her long hair between his fingers and gently rubbed them. He looked at his newly-bandaged leg and his bare chest and wondered how long he had been asleep. He pulled himself up, careful not disturb Alaina, and then gently laid her down on the bed. The world whirled around him as his body straightened and he knew that he must have had a fever and been a sleep for a considerable amount of time. He made it to the hammock and pulled himself up, almost instantly falling asleep again.

When a faint knocking sound was heard at the door a short time later, Alexander was first to awaken. He slowly and awkwardly swung himself out of the hammock, silently landed on his good leg and hobbled over to the door.

Ian stood at the door holding soup and drinking water as the door opened. "For you," the young man said. "Your wife?"

Alexander motioned to the bed. "Sleeping."

Ian looked in briefly and then was gone. Alexander put on a clean shirt and sat on the bed next to Alaina, pulling a stray strand of hair out of her face. She had her hands curled under her face and her lips were formed into a pout, but the movement on the bed had interrupted her sound sleep and she lazily opened her eyes and saw Alexander looking down at her.

She immediately sat up. "How long have you been up?"

"Here," he said handing her the soup. "Long enough to have had a visitor."

"Ian?"

"Is that his name? He was out of here pretty quick, so we didn't get a chance to exchange introductions."

"Did you frighten him off?"

"I didn't say a word," Alexander offered, raising his eyebrow. "Why would you think I'd frighten him off?"

Alaina sighed. "Because you frighten everyone off."

"No, I don't think I did. He was concerned enough about your well-being to make sure you were okay before handing over what looks to be some sort of soup. I wouldn't eat it if I were you, though."

"He probably saved your life, you know. He stole medicine from the doctor and brought us food and water for the last two days."

"You told someone I was sick?"

"I not only told him, I showed him," she said, not feeling guilty for her decision. "He looked at your leg and knew exactly what to do."

"Alaina, you could have gotten us both killed. He's just a boy; he could have told someone and they could have killed you, among other things."

His voice was becoming ever quieter and Alaina knew he was very angry, but she wasn't about to back down. She got up at the same time he did and stood facing him, hands on her hips. "It was risking my life, or you dying for sure. You had a high fever and I wasn't about to have your life on my conscience. Besides, nothing happened except that you got better, thanks to Ian." She didn't care if many considered him a dangerous man, not to be angered but handled carefully. She wasn't about to back down. Alaina could see Alexander was trying to suppress a smirk and it made her all the more angry.

"Do you know you are even more beautiful when you're angry? I might have to keep you angry all the time."

"You're doing a good job of that so far," she said. "Now that you're better, I'll go thank Ian myself, since you seem incapable of showing gratitude."

"You will stay away from that boy the rest of

the trip, do you understand?" His voice sounded cool and commanding as he spoke each word slowly for emphasis.

"You are..."

He raised his hand. "You will not disobey me in this."

"Just watch me," she said, walking toward the door.

"Do you wish to put his life at risk any more than he already has?" he warned.

She whirled around facing him again. "What do you mean? You're better now; no one will dare hurt us."

"Alaina, these men are dangerous. I don't know how many men Mustafa sent after you. He has people everywhere. He has his own international terrorist group and it's growing all the time. You're just a small part in his plans, but also the most recent sting, and to him personally. Trust me when I tell you that you are in danger until I can get you to Germany and you can change your name and live anonymously."

"I don't understand..." she started to say, but as she saw Alexander grab for the wall to get his balance, she quickly went to his aid.

"Lie down. You're still not well." She helped him lie down on the bed and watched as he closed his eyes, his breathing barely discernible. "Alexander?" she asked softly. As she received no answer, she repeated his name. "Please be all right," she pleaded, stroking her hand over his forehead. "Don't leave me."

The raw fear in her voice and the gentle touch of her hand finally penetrated Alexander's drifting senses, and in his semi-conscious state, all he could do to comfort her was put his arm around her waist and pull her next to him.

Alaina tried to get up, but his arm was locked around her waist and she knew it was useless to persist. Instead, she pulled herself closer to form better to his body, closed her eyes, and with the reassuring feeling that he would not die, allowed herself to relax for the first time in forty hours. With the knowledge that he was keeping her safe once more, she fell asleep with a smile on her lips.

Some days later, as Alaina watched Alexander walking in a small circle around the tiny room exercising his now-healing leg, she debated bringing up the subject of Ian again. Somehow they had to find some way to repay him for his mission of mercy. Alexander hadn't seen it that way, but as a way for Ian to act out his feelings of infatuation and play the hero to Alaina. Even if that were the case, Alaina felt it was her obligation to return his good deed. "Could we just discuss Ian one more time?" she appealed.

He continued walking. "Alaina, I promise I will do whatever lies in my power to help Ian's future look brighter than it does presently. Will that suffice?"

Alaina felt so happy that she flung herself at him with her whole body, knowing he would catch her. "Thank you," she said placing a kiss on his cheek. "Now I won't have to worry about finding a way to sneak him off this ship when we land."

"Is that what you had in mind?"

She was going to answer when he held his finger to her lips.

"On second thought, don't answer that. I'd rather not even know." He put her down and continued walking the stiffness out of his leg.

"Tell me what the people are like in Italy," she said, flopping herself down on the bed. Now with her worries about Ian resolved, life had become exciting again.

"You'll meet some tomorrow. This morning I radioed ahead to have some of my employees waiting for us."

# Chapter 7

They had walked the horses off the ship and stood on the dock. New smells, sights and sounds attacked Alaina's senses, but she remained next to Alexander patiently as he held Pegasus and she held Lady.

She watched as a tall man dressed in jeans, a blue cotton shirt and a large cowboy hat greeted Alexander, and then touched his hat briefly as he greeted Alaina. "Pleasure to meet you," he said in a lazy sort-of drawl that Alaina had never heard before, but that was not at all unpleasant.

He took the reins of both horses as Alexander explained, "Tony's from the ranch in Wyoming. He'll take the horses there today. When you settle in the right place, you can send for her later." Alexander was watching her and Alaina realized he was waiting for her to say something. He had stated it, yet he wasn't making the final decision for her.

"Take good care of her," she said to Tony, and watched as he led the horses away.

"Let me get some business out of the way and I'll be right back to introduce you to someone I think you'll like," Alexander said.

Alaina watched Alexander walk into the distance where a few men, all dressed very elegantly in dark colored suits, stepped forward to shake his hand and wait to hear instructions from him. They looked so different from the men she had grown up with. They didn't wear *thobes;* even their way of standing was different.

She also noticed a woman with them, wearing a pretty yellow dress that fluttered in the wind exposing her legs, and a matching hat she held to her head with a white-gloved hand. Her dark auburn hair shone in the morning sun and her beautiful face, enhanced with cosmetics, smiled radiantly. She seemed very familiar with Alexander as she stood smiling boldly at him.

Alaina turned her attention away from them, wanting the sudden stabbing pain in her heart to go away, knowing it had something to do with the way that woman kept looking at Alexander.

There were many cars parked along the harbor and in the distance the road was filled with them as far as she could see. In amazement, she looked at the many people around her, especially the women who were adorned in beautiful clothes and not covered from head to foot in black—some women were even driving!

She heard a woman's laugh and her attention focused back on Alexander and the woman, who were now walking toward her. She looked so refined and so very beautiful that Alaina suddenly felt inadequate.

Alexander pulled away from the woman and introduced her to Alaina. "Alaina, this is Sofia. She works for Maxwell Enterprises here in Italy, and I've asked her to help you with some shopping while you're here. She knows the better boutiques and shops to visit for your new wardrobe."

Sofia took Alaina's hand gently and smiled at her. There was warmth in her gaze, not hostility, as she had expected. "It's nice to meet you, Alaina. So you are going to Germany? We must find you beautiful clothes to show everyone in Germany how very fashionable we are in Italy." Alaina couldn't help responding with a smile and decided she liked this woman. "Let's get going right away, before the stores close at one. We will have fun together, no?"

Alexander waved them off. "You two have fun shopping. I have some business to take care of, but I'll meet you at one-thirty at Anthony's for lunch, and you can show me what you've bought."

Alaina followed Sofia to the waiting car. "You can drive?" she asked Sofia.

"Some might tell you otherwise, but I think I do all right." Sofia winked at her and Alaina watched carefully how she started the car and put it into gear. She would learn to drive soon, she promised herself. It didn't seem very hard. She looked out of the window and immediately became enthralled by all the new sights and sounds of the city, the bustle and scramble of the main shopping street.

"How far are we from Rome?"

"Only about fifty kilometers, but I know where to shop right here in our little town." They pulled along a small back alley and Sofia parked her little car.

"You will like this store, Alaina. They have the latest fashions from Milan and Paris." They got out of the car and entered a small boutique through what appeared the back door. The boutique had dresses thrown over chairs and the counter, and she saw several women briskly walking around with material and pins.

An exquisitely dressed older woman appeared out of a back room and, recognizing Sofia, hugged her. "Sofia, how wonderful it is to see you again," she said warmly in Italian.

The older woman looked at Alaina and smiled genuinely, making Alaina feel welcome, even though she felt totally out of place dressed as she was. "You bring me a friend, yes?" she asked, taking Alaina's hand.

Alaina was about to answer when Sofia explained, "She doesn't speak Italian. Maria, this is Alaina." Then Sofia switched to Italian and added, "She'll need everything from underwear to evening gowns, and," she paused to let the next words sink in, "Alexander said spare no expense. It is on the Maxwell expense account."

"Ah," Maria sighed, looking with new interest at Alaina, her eyes reflecting a glint of understanding. She turned back to Sofia and asked, "How much time do I have?"

"Three days."

"Three days! I will need to hire extra help," Maria lamented as she quickly and expertly took off Alaina's shirt and started taking Alaina's measurements. "What a figure," she mumbled to herself and then added to Sofia, "Just look at her body, so young and firm, no?"

Sofia said nothing.

Alaina felt naked and vulnerable standing in the shop with close to nothing on, while two women discussed her body. She had wanted to tell them she understood and spoke Italian fluently, but now was too embarrassed to mention it. She turned from them, looking at the many dresses around the store, afraid they would see the blush that was creeping up her neck.

Maria went through a few of her dresses on the rack, but saw Alaina's eyes wandering toward a blue satin dress adorning a mannequin. She smiled and agreed with Alaina's choice. "The girl has excellent taste—expensive taste," Maria said, laughing with delight to Sofia. She called for assistance from the back of the shop and two girls came running forward. "Undress the mannequin quickly, and help me."

The two women obeyed and brought the dress to her. While they were dressing her, Alaina tried hard to see what they were doing and move with them so as not to be stabbed by the loose pins. As the dress was finally on her, Maria came forward and started adjusting the pins and needles until the dress fit like a second skin. When it came to her bust line, Maria shook her head and then let out the seams. "She does not lack here either, no?" she commented to no one in particular. "What I would do for such a figure," Maria continued as she worked. "And look at those eyes, no? And this long hair. With my clothes, she will be irresistible to any man, yes?" She was talking to herself and no one answered her—no one had time. The two girls were busy showing Alaina more dresses, which Alaina learned had just arrived from Milan.

Two hours and many outfits later, Sofia looked at her watch. "It's almost one and Alexander will be waiting," she said, putting down her cappuccino and getting up from the couch she had been lounging on. "We'll continue after lunch."

"I have her measurements. I will pick out some slips and undergarments of the finest silk while you are gone," Maria said to Sofia.

"See you soon," Sofia said to Maria in English.

Alaina dressed quickly and said, "Thank you," in English.

From the boutique, they drove through the narrow streets, then out to an open boulevard. "What a wonderful city!" Alaina said. "Look at the water fountain, and those sculptures on the buildings. And the man there selling hats—he's got a monkey! Oh please can we stop? I'd love to see the monkey!"

"You'll have to buy a hat first." Sofia said laughing as she pulled the car onto the sidewalk not far from the man.

Alaina looked quickly at his selection and picked a large straw sombrero. She had some American dollars in her pocket and handed the man a twenty dollar bill. The man seemed very pleased with his sale and the monkey climbed down his arm and stood before Alaina. He took off his little red hat as if to say thank you and when Alaina held out her hand, he quickly shook it and then ran back to the man.

"We really must go or we'll be late, Alaina." Sofia said.

As they got back into the car, Alaina told her, "I love animals, don't you?"

"Not especially," she replied.

They parked next to a small cafe where Alexander was seated reading the *Wall Street Journal*. He stood up, surprised to see Alaina in the same clothes she had left in. "Where are the clothes?" he asked Sofia.

Sofia took his arm intimately, snuggling up against him, her breasts pushed into his arm, and said in English, "Everything has to be altered to fit her." She switched to Italian with Alexander and very softly purred, "Oh, Alexander, you do not have to leave so soon this time, do you? You will not want to leave before we've had another weekend together. You remember, during your last trip, it was incredible, no?"

"Sofia, behave yourself," he said, firmly untangling her arm from his and looking incisively into her eyes. "We discussed this before. That was an exceptional weekend, yes, but we are not meant for each other and we both know that."

Alaina wanted to look away, but couldn't. She had seen that look in his eyes before, it was cold and unfeeling and she could see Sofia was disappointed. "And I don't think Joe would be too happy," he added, watching Sofia closely.

"You know about Joe?" Sofia's eyes became large with surprise.

"He stopped by the office to inform me you two were getting married in six months." Before she could reply, he added, "Sofia, since you are using Italian to speak to me privately, I presume you are not aware that Alaina understands and speaks Italian?"

Sofia whirled around to see if Alexander spoke the truth. The blush on Alaina's face, along with her averted eyes, was all she needed to know the answer. "Alaina, why didn't you say something in the boutique?"

Alaina looked from Alexander, whose lazy smile informed her that he found the situation rather amusing, to Sofia, whose blazing eyes flashed indignation and astonishment, making it clear she did not find the situation entertaining. Alaina straightened slightly, returning Sofia's indignant gaze, and explained, "I thought once you had already started talking about me, it would be as embarrassing to you as it was to me to realize I understood."

Sofia looked from Alaina to Alexander and frowned, realizing the joke was on her. "I'm sorry, Alaina. I guess I have been rather impolite, among other things."

Happy that the moment now rested on her answer, Alaina cheerfully said, "I forgive you. I'm so hungry, could we eat now?"

Alexander signaled to a man dressed in black

with a white apron, and he seated them near a large window overlooking the harbor. The man handed Alaina a small menu with many items she had never eaten before. Since she had never eaten at a restaurant before either, she wanted to try everything on the menu.

"I don't know what many of these things are."

Alexander explained everything on the menu.

"I want to try everything. Do you think I could try some of everything?"

"Maybe we can get them to give you a sampler's dish," Sofia suggested. She got up to speak with someone in another room.

"This is so exciting," Alaina said to Alexander. "I want to learn to drive as soon as possible and I want to see Rome! Did you see the fountains in the squares here? Of course you have, you work here sometimes. Have you ever been to Rome?"

Sofia came back before Alexander could answer her.

"You must save room for ice cream, Alaina. It's the best in the world!" Sofia told her.

Alexander found Alaina completely enchanting. He watched while she finished her third glass of yet another wine, her long blond hair flowing over her shoulders and magnificent blue eyes sparkling with the laughter that now touched her lips. This was another side of her he didn't know, and he found himself captivated by the beauty of her laugh and her infectious joy over even the small things, things he'd grown oblivious to. How could he ever let her go? Germany was too far away from New York.

They brought out some hazelnut ice cream and Alaina had never tasted anything like it before. She ordered seconds.

"If you continue eating like that, you'll be too fat to take anywhere," Alexander teased.

"I don't care," Alaina said. "It's all so wonderful." She paused and put her spoon down. More seriously, she said, "Thank you."

Alexander's usually cool eyes were now warm as he looked at Alaina, and he splurged his wickedly handsome smile on her.

"Alaina, you'll have to tell me about your journey here," Sofia said, interrupting the moment.

"Maybe some other time," Alexander said. "We need to get some paperwork out of the way first. Why don't you take the rest of the day off, Sofia, and tomorrow morning you can continue with your shopping."

After lunch, Alexander and Alaina drove to the home of the American Consulate General along the beach. "We need to get you a visa to enter the United States," Alexander explained. "The only problem I see is that you don't have a Swedish passport. We'll see what we can do with the paperwork you do have."

"Don't I need a visa for Germany?"

"No."

"When am I going to the United States?"

"I just thought it's better to get it settled now. You may want to visit the States in the future."

Alaina soon realized there was a long-standing relationship between Alexander and the consulate general, who made a few phone calls. Soon Alaina had paperwork allowing her entry into the United States.

"It's getting late and I'd like to get us checked into the hotel. Our luggage is waiting for us there," Alexander said as he escorted her to the car.

Alaina was too tired to think about Germany now, and as she sat in the car she felt, of all things, sad. She knew she should be happy and content with everything she'd seen and done and how nice everyone had been to her; even Alexander had been extremely easy to be with today, yet she couldn't shake the feeling of unfairness in the world. She couldn't stop thinking about Ian.

Alexander seemed to sense she was unhappy. "What's wrong, Alaina?" he asked tenderly, but she shook her head.

"Tell me," he tried again, taking her hand in his own and adding softly, "You can tell me anything."

She decided to start diplomatically, "I don't want to sound ungrateful, but...oh, never mind." He had been so kind to her she couldn't ask him for more now.

"You're pouting about something."

"Am I?"

"Yes, and I want to know what is bothering you."

"Must I tell you everything?"

"Yes," he said firmly, but was smiling when he said it.

Alaina turned away from his smile and looked out the window. "I was just thinking of Ian. I feel so selfish having received so much when I know Ian has nothing, not even a chance to get off that terrible ship."

Alexander let go of her hand as he parked the car outside the hotel. He noticed tears glittering in her eyes and was beginning to understood what a great capacity for empathy and compassion she had, making her all the more dear to him, especially when in his own world, hostilities and strife dominated every aspect of his life. "Would you be happy if Ian were off the ship?"

She nodded and Alexander smiled. He was known around the world as a hard businessman, a ruthless tycoon without a conscience, and yet here he sat next to a young woman, ready to do anything just to hear her laugh again. "Come on, let's get some sleep. You'll feel better in the morning."

He picked up the keys at the desk and walked Alaina to her room. He put the key in the lock of the suite's door and said, "I'm not the ungrateful person you think I am, Alaina. And I strongly dislike owing anyone my life, so I usually return a favor as quickly as possible."

Alaina could not believe her eyes when Alexander opened the door and saw Ian sitting on a couch in the front room, looking into some kind of box with lights radiating from it. "Ian!" she cried, running forward to hug him.

Ian, seemingly embarrassed at her tight embrace, glanced sheepishly toward Alexander who was coming toward them. Alexander allowed Alaina to pull him into the embrace and he put one arm around Alaina's waist and the other on the boy's shoulder.

"Oh, Ian, this is so wonderful. I can't believe...How long have you been here?" Alaina asked Ian excitedly.

"Since this morning, and I've learned more today in a few hours watching this thing than in my whole life!" He pointed to the television.

Alexander laughed. "But what you see there is not the real world. Don't get hooked. I have work for you tomorrow."

"What is that thing?" Alaina asked. She walked up to the television and touched it. "Who is inside?"

Ian answered proudly, "Well, this is television. I saw it once before when I was given leave off the ship. I saw a movie. Have you ever seen a movie?"

"A movie?" she sighed. "There is so much in your world I don't understand or know about," she told Alexander. "But I do know now that you have a good heart."

"Don't count on it," Alexander said as he signaled Ian to come with him. "I'll be back shortly. I need to show Ian to his room."

Ian was free and Alaina realized that is how she felt herself. She looked around the room as she spun for joy and then saw an open door leading to another room exactly like her own. She knew it was probably Alexander's room. She saw another door next to it and wondered what it could lead to. She opened it and saw a beautiful bathroom as large as a front room at home. She had never seen so much polished marble in one room.

"You like it?" Alexander asked softly close to her ear.

She jumped, not having heard him enter the room. "It's all so different and new," she answered.

He put his arms around her waist and pulled her gently into him. "You'll get used to it soon enough and wonder how you ever managed without it."

She turned around in his arms. "Thank you for what you did for Ian." He was looking at her lips and then into her eyes. Alaina saw intensity entering his eyes and she knew she had to put distance between them. She wiggled loose from his embrace and headed for the couch.

"What did you mean by Ian having to work tomorrow?"

"Ian and I talked earlier, and we've decided the best thing for him is to go to school. He has to sit down tomorrow and figure out what school he wants to go to. I've explained about the top universities in this country, England and the United States, and I'll pay for whatever degree he wants, but in the meantime he'll have to finish high school. You're going to have to make some of those decisions yourself soon." Alexander came and sat down beside Alaina on the couch.

She backed away slightly from him.

"Alaina, why are you pulling away?"

"Why do you say that?" she asked.

"I know you. I can tell."

"How can you tell?"

"The same way I can tell when an executive of mine walks in the room and he feels I'll be unhappy with what he has to say, or when it's time to either make the deal or walk away." Alaina frowned. "And because you haven't been mad at me once this afternoon," he teased.

She felt confused. She was engaged to Devon Maxwell, who was Alexander's employer and worse, a relative, and she couldn't allow feelings to develop for Alexander. She thought Alexander wouldn't want her to, desire was obvious in his eyes.

She was not so naive she didn't know that desire and love were two different things.

She knew so little about either man. Did either of them have any other women in their lives? She expressed her thoughts softly, "Are there other women in your life, besides Sofia?"

For a fleeting moment he seemed taken aback by the question. "If you're wondering if there will be any more scenes like the one you witnessed this afternoon, I can't say for sure. Women are certainly unpredictable." He got up and headed for the door. "But if you're asking if there is one woman in my life, the answer is no," he added coolly.

"Michelle?"

He stopped with his back still to her.

"I'm sorry. It's just that you had a dream..."

"Michelle no longer exists in my life," he said. "I do not want her name mentioned again." He left without turning around.

Alaina wished she could take back her words. She knew she had taken a chance by bringing up the past, but only now realized how bad the odds had been. With tears stinging her eyes, she pulled back the covers and sadly climbed into the big cold bed, her body aching with exhaustion. But her conscience wouldn't let her sleep, not for a very long time at least. She had heard the pain in his voice, underneath the anger.

The next morning the telephone by Alaina's bed rang. "This is the front desk, mademoiselle," Alaina heard as she picked up the receiver. "I have a message to awaken you at eight this morning and Monsieur Alexander has instructed me to give you the following message, 'Sofia will be by at nine to take you shopping. I will be back late tonight, so don't wait for me.'"

Is this a bad dream? Alaina thought. How could she possibly spend another day shopping? She quickly got dressed and knocked on the door down the hallway.

"Ian? Ian?" she called. "It's me, Alaina."

"Alaina, what are you doing?" Ian asked as he opened the door.

She was glad Ian was already dressed. "I'm to be pinched and poked today by at least a dozen woman trying to fit me into clothes I don't want, and I can't bear the thought of it when there's a whole new world to investigate out there. I was hoping you'd join me on a little journey."

"Alaina, I'd like to go, but I'm to decide what education I want and what to do with the rest of my life. As that is a rather weighty matter, I should probably do it first." Ian smirked at her.

"Why don't you let me help you?"

"How can you help me?"

"Well, I'm an excellent reader and I could read through everything for you and then we can discuss it."

"I'm to discuss it with Alexander this evening."

"Fine, Ian, if you don't want to go with me, that's OK, I'm going anyway. If you see Sofia, just tell her I had other plans today."

"Alaina, do you think this is such a good idea? It might be dangerous to go alone."

"Ian, am I always to wait around for someone to take me somewhere or tell me what I can or cannot do? It's different here from where I come from, and I want to know all about it. I saw women yesterday out alone and they looked perfectly fine."

"Alexander won't..."

"Alexander is busy with his own affairs," she interrupted, "and I don't intend to be pushed around from one person to the next to take care of me. I can take care of myself. My foster grandmother went to school in Rome and she told me many stories about many places, including Rome, which Sofia told me is only fifty kilometers from here. I want to see it before I'm transported to Germany to see my cousin, if he's been located yet." As she said these words, she felt a strong resentment rise inside her that she hadn't known existed before. She wanted to have family, yet she was afraid she'd be trapped again and someone else would control her life.

"Wait, I'll go with you. Alexander shouldn't have left you on your own."

"Only if you want to Ian. I don't want you along as a protector, just a friend." He nodded seriously. "Please bring your books. I can help you and it might be better if you had something to tell Alexander tonight." She didn't want Ian to be in trouble with Alexander.

Two hours later the two descended from a bus. Alaina unconsciously put her hand on Ian's shoulder as if to steady herself. "Can you believe this? Rome! I want to see everything, Michelangelo's paintings, the school my grandmother attended and..."

Ian laughed. "Okay, Okay. Where do you want to start? Who is this Michael Angelo?"

"Oh, Ian, I'm so excited I'm here, and I am going to show you everything I've ever read or heard about, and then I want to eat."

"How would it be if we ate first since I'm starving?"

"Look, there's a man selling something. Let's get something there and eat on the way," Alaina said, grabbing his hand and running across the square, scattering pigeons all around them.

Ian watched Alaina as she got directions and soon they entered the Sistine Chapel, where Alaina told him the history behind the paintings and art.

"Can you believe it? He finished in 1512, four years after he'd started, the same year the Fifth Lateran Council pronounced the 'Immortality of the Soul' dogma of the Church," Alaina said as she gazed at the ceiling of the chapel. "I'm sorry, Ian, I don't mean to go on so, this is just so wonderful, to see history come alive."

"You know, much of what you're saying I don't even understand," he acknowledged honestly. "Before today, I was hesitant about going to school. I wanted to make it on my own, but now I see how much there is to know, and how isolated I've been on a small ship all my life, with no knowledge of books."

"My adoptive mother had an indescribable love of books, so I was around them all my life. It was my only contact with the outside. I, too, was isolated growing up."

They heard bells ringing and Alaina thought it was one of the saddest sounds she'd ever heard. "Oh, I don't want to go yet," she said.

"I'm sorry too, but we have to leave now on the bus to make it back. Let's get some of that ice cream for the ride." They left arm in arm, Alaina feeling happy with their new found friendship that had been cemented by their adventure together.

# Chapter 8

Alexander sat in his office looking out the window over the harbor. The power and determination that radiated from him put people around him on edge. Only his closest associate and friend, who was now sitting in Alexander's office having a drink, was totally at ease with him.

"Seems I got here just in time. Brought you today's *New York Times*."

"You needed the week off, didn't you? Why didn't you take it?"

"Plans changed and I had nothing better to do." Rich said, twisting his glass. "So what's the story with the girl, Alex?"

"Alaina? I'm taking her to Germany next week to see if we can locate a cousin of hers. I've got calls in to the right people, I just haven't heard anything yet. I'm hoping to keep this low-key. I'd also like to give her a chance to think things through before we find her family. Maybe take her skiing, something happy in her life."

"If I were you, I'd consider going as soon as possible."

"Why is that?"

"Find the gossip column in the paper."

"You know I never read that stuff, Rich."

"But this time you might want to. It has to do with Alaina." Rich opened to the right page for him.

Alexander looked at the article which started off with the latest speculations on where he had been in the last two weeks and then stated they had discovered he had been playing desert bandit with a lovely blond whose name they had not yet discovered, but speculated she was an heiress to an oil fortune.

Alexander swore under his breath and threw the paper down. "You're right, we'll leave tomorrow. Take over for me again, old man," he said, gathering his briefcase and heading for the door. "And Rich, find out how they got the information regarding her oil connections."

Alexander picked up a message on the way out of the office. He read the message and then crumpled it up as he walked out, leaving Rich to wonder what it was all about.

As he entered the hotel lobby, Alexander looked at his watch and saw it was nine o'clock already. Ian and he would be having a late dinner, he thought, and sighed. He had not intended to have Ian wait so long, but then he wasn't even sure if Ian and Alaina were back yet. Sofia had left him the message that the two youngsters had asked directions from the hotel desk about which bus went to Rome and then had gotten on that bus. He felt like strangling Alaina for having gone off on her own. She was such an innocent in the world, but at least Ian had had enough sense to keep an eye on her. Ian had proven his intelligence and insight several times since their first meeting, and Alexander had great expectations for him should he want to pursue a career in the business world.

But at the moment, it seemed he suddenly had two orphans on his hands.

He caught sight of his 'two orphans,' laughing over some joke with the porter. He smiled despite his anger. His eyes caught Alaina's and he saw the sparkle of laughter in her eyes, but the smile that was on her lips started to fade as she saw him. Then, to his surprise, she bestowed a breath-taking smile on him as she started walking towards him, and he again found himself enchanted. She was such a contrast, innocent one moment and sensuous the next.

"Alexander, we missed you today. We had the most wonderful day, Ian and I. We went to Rome and visited the Sistine Chapel, among other sights," she said and took his arm. "I know you want to have dinner with Ian now, so I'll be running along. And, please don't be upset with Ian, it was all my fault he didn't stay here today looking over those dull books you left for him. I forced him to come along with me as my chaperone." She let go of his arm to leave them.

"Alaina," Alexander said, pulling her back. "I'd like to hear about your day before you leave. Why don't you have dinner with us, since I won't be discussing career goals with Ian tonight."

"Sir, I'm sorry..." Ian started apologizing, his serious expression telling Alexander he was feeling as though he had let him down.

Alexander lifted his hand to interrupt Ian, but kept his gaze on Alaina. Alaina knew he hadn't fallen for her excuse. "I'd also like to hear how the two of you got to Rome."

Just then the clerk from the front desk came and informed Alexander there was an emergency phone call. "Go ahead to the dining room and order. I'll be back," Alexander said. He went to the lobby and picked up the phone.

"Alexander," came Rich's voice through the phone. "We've got a major problem. I don't know what to make of it yet. Can you talk?"

"I'll be right over. Briefly, what are we dealing with?"

"Good thing you beefed up security when you returned. Our men just apprehended a suspect with enough TNT to blow this place up."

"Have you called the police?"

"No, I called you first."

"Good, don't inform them. Where are you keeping him?"

"Downstairs. Out of sight."

"Rich, double security again in every branch, worldwide. I have a feeling this is only the beginning."

"What's going on?"

"I'll be there in fifteen minutes. And Rich, this is need-to-know only."

Back in the hotel's restaurant, he said to Alaina and Ian, "My apologies, but I'm needed back at the office."

Alaina did not miss the coldness in his eyes and the hard set of his jaw. "Alexander, is everything all right?"

"It will be. Don't worry. Plan to leave for Germany tomorrow, Alaina. And Ian, sometime tonight I'll stop by your room and we'll discuss your plans, OK?" Ian nodded.

Alexander had a good idea what this was all about—Mustafa. He knew there was a reason they had gotten away so easily, and now he was beginning to understand what it was. Mustafa had gone to school in the West; he knew how to ruin a man financially, if that's what he wanted to do. Alexander also didn't put it past Mustafa to kill anyone who might get in his way.

He arrived at the office and met Rich. "The suspect's in here," Rich said, "but he's not talking. I think we could torture him to death before he would talk."

Alexander walked into the tiny room and looked at the man who would have blown his office sky high, giving no thought to how many people would have died.

The man showed no remorse and when Alexander came within range, he spit at him.

Alexander held back his security guards and sat down in front of the man. Alexander spoke Arabic. "I know of ways to torture a man that will make anything Mustafa does feel like a cold shower. But for right now, I'm not going to touch you. Instead, I'm going to have one of my men accompany you back to Saudi and release you into Mustafa's hands. He will also leak the information that you told me about Mustafa's plot. He will not appreciate failure—or a traitor."

The man started to say something, but Alexander got up and left the room.

"What did you say?" Rich asked Alexander.

"Basically, that we were escorting him back to his country to Mustafa's hands."

"What will Mustafa do to him? He looked scared to death."

"Nothing you'd want to know about. Have Jim escort him back. Make sure Jim understands that he is not to be seen, that he is only to get him off the boat and stash $20,000 into one of his pockets just before he gets off the ship. He'll be able to handle him. When Mustafa's men grab him and see the money, they'll believe he double-crossed them. I'm worried about Alaina, also. I don't think he wants her dead, but he might attempt to kidnap her. I'm taking her to Germany tomorrow, maybe she can disappear for a while."

Back at the hotel, he stopped to look in on Ian and discuss what Ian had in mind for his future.

He agreed with Ian that he should look around before deciding anything. "Rich can help you with anything you need and he will know where to contact me, should you need to reach me. And Ian, thank you for taking care of Alaina today."

"It was no bother," Ian said slowly. As Alexander started for the door, Ian blurted out, "Do you love her at all?"

Alexander raised an eyebrow at Ian's question. "Is that your business?" In the last twenty-four hours he had been asked more questions about his private life than in the past year. People generally knew better, but he was dealing with a youngster here, he thought. He walked back to Ian, who was now shuffling his feet. "She's young and refreshing, and intriguing, yes. Why do you ask?"

"Because I don't want you to hurt her."

Alexander walked to the door again and said softly before he shut it behind him, "You still have much to learn about women, Ian. Don't let them pull on your heart strings or you'll be the one left to bleed."

# Chapter 9

Alaina lay on Alexander's couch, waiting. She watched as he entered his room. As he was about to turn on the lamp on his desk, he hesitated. His actions told her he knew he was being watched. He moved away from the desk and casually walked toward the balcony in the dark, waiting.

"Alexander," she said, wanting him to know it was her.

Alaina's voice couldn't be mistaken and he relaxed. He turned on the lamp. "What are you doing here?"

"I was worried about you. I knew the phone call was bad news."

"What?"

"When you are angry, the color of your eyes change, they become clear blue, almost gray. When you are more relaxed, they turn almost green."

Alexander's shoulders shook with laughter. "And when my eyes are red, what does that mean?"

"You don't have to believe me, but I always know when you are angry by your eyes."

"There are other ways you can tell, too, which you will soon experience if you don't get back to your room."

"I'm not afraid of you. " Alaina raised her chin ever so slightly.

"That's your mistake."

"I know you're not angry with me now because your eyes are almost green." But she also saw something else appear in his eyes that made her feel suddenly naked, even though her body was covered with her robe. "But I will go anyway," she said quickly, backing up towards the door.

"Good, I'll walk you to your room," he said. Before Alaina could say anything, and before they got to her room, Alexander made her crouch down with him. Then she saw what Alexander had seen immediately. The door to the corridor was open and so was her balcony door. Someone had been in her room earlier. "Maybe we should leave tonight," he said. "Can you get ready?" She nodded. "I'll wait here with you while you dress and pack."

"Does this have to do with you or me? Am I in danger still? From Mustafa?"

"It could just be a thief who picked your room to rob. I'm not sure. But I don't want to take any chances; we're still too close to Mustafa's back yard."

They departed without word to anyone.

"What are you doing?" Alaina asked as she sat in his car and he got down on the ground to look under it.

"Just checking that everything is all right," he assured her.

"What about Ian?"

"He knows what he'll be doing. You can call him tomorrow if you like." He started the car and added, "You might as well sleep while it's still dark. I'll wake you if anything exciting happens."

The hours passed. Alaina slept as Alexander drove. As the first light of morning streamed in through the windows of their car, she awakened slowly. "Good morning," Alexander said good naturedly. "You really sleep quite soundly, you know. You missed the traffic accident, the wild boars that attacked us, and..."

"Wild boars?" For a moment she thought he was serious, but then saw the smirk building on his face and she swung a punch at him, but laughed with him. "I guess I was tired." She sat up and looked around her. She gasped as she saw the giant mountain peaks surrounding them, imposing and magnificently inspiring. "Alexander, what are those?"

"The Alps."

"They're..." she couldn't find the word to describe them, "majestic," she whispered. A feeling of awe and respect swept through her from the pit of her stomach and for some reason she couldn't understand, she felt like crying.

Alexander watched her as she wiped a tear running down her cheek.

"I agree, and as we get closer, they'll become even more impressive, especially in the small town we'll be staying in."

"What's it called?"

"Garmisch-Partenkirchen. It's on the German border. I thought we could take a day, relax, go skiing before we start looking for your cousin."

"Skiing? I've never skied before, either."

"You'll love it, as all good Swedes should."

They drove through Austria and several mountain passes before arriving late that afternoon. They checked into a hotel and then took a stroll through town. As they walked through the valley, the mountains stood, overpowering and towering, around them on all sides, and the small shops and cafes that lined the streets beckoned them. The winter season was just getting into swing but already skiers were coming from around the world.

"Do you know how to ski?" Alaina asked.

Alexander nodded and seeing her delight, asked if she would like to learn. "Tonight?"

"Let's get you outfitted and then I have some business to attend to." They walked into the nearest ski shop and got her fitted with boots, bindings, skis and the clothes to go along with them. Alexander paid with nine 100 deutsche marks and told them to deliver them to their hotel. They walked the rest of the way back to the hotel talking about the beautiful scenery surrounding them.

Alaina's room felt warm and cozy with a fire glowing in the corner. While Alexander attended to his business, Alaina tried to call Ian, but before she could leave a message at the hotel, she heard a knock at the door. She gave Alexander a sunny smile.

"Are you ready to go?" he asked, smiling in return.

"Ready."

The next three hours went by quickly for Alaina. She fell down, covered in snow for the umpteenth time, still smiling and more determined than ever to get it right. "I want to try a bigger hill," she said, taking Alexander's hand. He had stayed by her side constantly, always there to pick her up, brush her off and make sure she was still in one piece, just as he was now. "I get stuck in this same spot of ice every time."

"All right, but after we get you warmed up. Your lips are turning blue," he teased. They went to a little cafe on the edge of town close to the gondola.

"Are there towns like this in America?"

"You mean with mountains like these?"

She nodded. "Where one can ski down into

the village and eat and then take a ride back to the top?"

"In the Rocky Mountains, there are mountains similar to these. There are a few ski places similar to this, but not quite like this town. For the last few years I've been contemplating investing in a valley in the Canadian Rockies which has the potential to look much like this."

Alaina looked excited. "You would start from the beginning and design a town?"

He nodded, not missing her interest. "Does such a venture appeal to you?"

"Oh yes! I've studied much about ancient architecture and have often, in my fantasies back in the desert, dreamed up whole cities."

"I would have thought young girls would dream of princes on white horses and living happily ever after."

Alaina looked for signs that he was teasing her, but he gave her an unreadable look. "Am I so different from girls in the West?"

Now it was Alexander's turn to be perplexed at the change in conversation. Looking into her magnificent eyes, now pleading for acceptance, his blood started pumping faster throughout his body, which was now reacting on its own, and said in a low voice, "Yes, you're very different from any woman I've ever met."

Alaina blushed slightly as she understood the meaning of his words, and looked away for a moment. She had to change the direction the conversation was headed. "What do American girls do when they get out of school? Mother told me most girls as well as boys go to universities."

Alexander smiled at her, fascinated at how quickly she could change the subject. For some reason he didn't understand, he wanted to see her blush again. "Don't try to change the subject, Alaina. I think you're perfect the way you are."

Alaina wondered if the tea was contributing to the warm sensation she felt inside or if it was only his intimate compliment. "Alexander..."

"I like the sound of my name on your lips," he said, his eyes becoming darker and his tone changing from teasing to husky.

Alaina felt a surge of thrilling shivers throughout her body and her heart started slamming in her throat, nearly choking her as she watched him, not being able to turn away, yet embarrassed to keep looking into his darkened eyes. She held her breath, watching him move closer.

As he watched her lips, she unwittingly licked them.

A waiter interrupted the moment by bringing more tea.

Alexander straightened, his face becoming void of feeling. She suddenly exhaled, only now realizing she had stopped breathing. She understood he wore a mask most of the time, yet she knew there was more underneath. His cool expression was all a facade, and she wanted to understand him more than ever. What had happened that he had built such defenses around his soul?

"You were asking?" he asked, still smiling, but in his eyes she saw he was just as incorrigible as ever.

"I'll get specific then," she said, ignoring his smile. "What opportunities would there be for me in New York?"

Alexander watched her for a minute before realizing she was serious. "That depends on you, and what you would like to do."

"Are there many women in government or in corporations? What could I do in New York?"

Alexander sat forward again, "What did you have in mind?"

"Why are you answering every one of my questions with a question?"

"Sorry," he said genuinely. "A business tactic."

"Should I go to school?"

"I think you're probably qualified for most any job a woman holds in Maxwell Enterprises," he said, "but you tell me what you're interested in and I'll try to find the position."

"I would like to be a part of building a town such as this."

"Not a bad idea. And I understand you have the money to invest in it."

"What do you mean?"

"All your mother's holdings go to you now. You are a very wealthy young woman.'

"Where is this money?" she asked, surprised.

"It's been deposited in Swiss bank accounts. You have the bankbooks in your possession."

She narrowed her eyes in disbelief. "Why haven't you told me before?"

"I wasn't sure myself what provisions your mother made for you until a few hours ago. That was some of the business I wanted to check into. Now that you know you have money to take care of you, do you still want to work for Maxwell Enterprises or do you want a different lifestyle?"

"I'm not sure," she answered.

"I see," he said flatly.

She looked at him and smiled. "I might build the town myself and give Devon Maxwell some competition."

Alexander sat back and laughed out loud, his rich deep voice carrying through the restaurant. People around them stopped their conversations and looked at the handsome couple who were now standing up. Alexander looked down at Alaina, his eyes filled with fondness, and, taking her hand, kissed it. "I'll look forward to it," he said, and bestowed upon her a breathtaking, charming smile.

They returned to the hotel and after changing into more comfortable clothing, both stood in front of a blazing fire warming themselves. Alexander ordered some wine that was sweet and smooth and made Alaina feel happy.

Alexander pulled her closer to him and Alaina once again didn't know how she should feel. She had spent so much time with this man, and yet knew so little about him. Whenever he started becoming playful with her, he became a dark, mysterious stranger, one she found threatening. Yet at the same time, he was her knight in shining armor, who had come to her rescue.

Where was Devon Maxwell? Why didn't he come for her so she could straighten out her life? When was she finally going to meet the man who was to be her husband, should he accept?

"Alexander..." she started.

Without warning he gathered her into his arms, and though her mind warned her to flee, she couldn't move. As his lips seized her mouth, her body reacted out of instinct, giving in to the weakness he stimulated in her.

A half-groan, half-laugh was wrung from him as he felt her arms tighten around his neck. "You are incredible," he said in a husky, tender voice, and then lowered his lips to her eyes, her ears, and then down her neck. Alaina jumped in surprise at the sensations assaulting her body, her entire nervous system raging.

"Don't pull away, sweetheart," he whispered hoarsely.

Responding to the harsh need in his voice, she kissed him, her tongue touching his lips this time, and when she felt him quiver, her instinct told her she was turning the tables. She felt his heart pounding against her breast, and she could feel his control dissolving. Her mouth melted into his and she kissed him with her own unleashed passion, previously kept so tightly under control, now too raging to restrain.

His hand reached for and cupped her breast possessively, and her body reacted instantly. Startled, she abruptly pushed him away, gasping for breath and control. "Oh, please," she said. "Please don't do this to me. I don't know what you want."

"I want you," he said still staring at her full, bruised lips. "And you want me." He continued kissing her before she could protest.

She pushed him away again. "Please, we cannot. I'm still engaged to Devon Maxwell until I hear otherwise from him." Her voice quivered as she tried to calm her heart.

Alexander took a step forward and then hesitated, his eyes clouding over and becoming unreadable again. "As you wish," he said, suddenly distant and cool.

Alaina felt like screaming. Her body cried out in what felt like pain, as if it needed something more, something she had no knowledge of, something she was certain Alexander could give her, yet also knowing she couldn't have it.

Only he had ever made her feel this way. How was she ever going to work with him in New York? She voiced her concerns unthinkingly. "Maybe I shouldn't go with you to New York."

"But you wanted to meet Devon Maxwell."

"Couldn't I go out to Wyoming where he lives," she said walking to the couch.

"No, not yet," Alexander said.

"So you've talked to him recently?" Alaina asked confused. "Why do you keep things from me?"

"There is something I need to tell you now. I'm glad you're considering New York, because I have some bad news." His eyes expressed a sadness, and a kindness that had not been there before, almost pity.

She knew then what he was to tell her. "My cousin in Germany is not there," she said. She watched as he slowly came to her and put his arms around her. "There is no one then," she whispered.

Alexander heard the distress in her voice and pulled her head to his chest, stroking her hair. "I'm sorry, Alaina" He hadn't expected such sadness and contemplated telling her the truth about her cousin, that he lived in Sweden now. But he quickly decided that this was the best way. He needed to keep watch over her.

"What just happened will not happen again, not unless you know that's what you want. You'll be safe working in New York. In fact, I've been thinking of hiring a bodyguard for you."

She had always known that he would not be able to stay with her constantly, as he had in the past few weeks, and this saddened her even more than realizing she had no family. "I need to pack if we're leaving tomorrow," she said softly, waiting for his response.

He only nodded at her and then stared into the roaring fire.

# Chapter 10

The limousine swerved violently through the crowded streets of New York City and Alaina held on to the door for leverage. She glanced at Alexander for reassurance, but he seemed involved in some documents that had been waiting for him in the limousine, and seemed not to notice anything unusual about the ride. She didn't think the drive from the airport was so bad, maybe because she had been too excited, but now she sighed and realized this must be normal in New York. She looked out the window and saw mountains of lifeless concrete, thousands of people walking the streets, and narrow roads of pavement and steel. She wondered what kept people in such a place. She wondered if anything could ever keep her here.

Alexander saw her holding the door as she watched out the window. "He's not the greatest driver," he commented softly.

Alaina looked from the window to him now. He was dressed in a black business suit that was perfectly tailored and fell over his tall, broad frame elegantly. "Why do you have him as a driver then?"

"Because that's his side job. He's my bodyguard," he said, looking back down at his papers again.

"I wouldn't think you needed a bodyguard," she said, wondering how dangerous New York could be.

"When I don't have him around I seem to get stabbed by captivating young women," he said, his eyes twinkling.

She smiled and looked out the window again, thinking how long ago that seemed and how much had happened since then. And now she was in America, and maybe soon she would meet the man she was to marry. She didn't know exactly when she had started feeling resentment for this arranged marriage, or the guilt that accompanied her resentment, but she wanted to be totally free and in control of her own life. Her dreams and fantasies of Devon Maxwell being her savior knight no longer existed. Devon Maxwell was no longer real to her, but Alexander was becoming more real with every passing moment.

The limousine pulled into a parking garage and onto a private parking deck. Alaina followed Alexander and noticed the driver stayed close behind her. Alexander placed a key into an elevator panel and soon she was riding up over forty stories, quickly enough to hurt her ears. "Does Devon Maxwell own this whole building?" she asked incredulously.

"Yes, but Maxwell Enterprises uses only on the top 15 floors. The rest we rent out."

The door opened and they stepped out, leaving the driver behind. "Good to see you back, sir," a gentleman said loudly as they walked by his office. "Welcome back," an older woman said, who was sitting just outside his office and was apparently his secretary. She got up promptly with a steno pad in hand and followed them into the office, shutting the door behind her.

Alexander gave her the papers he had been

reading on the drive over and said, "Excellent, give it to George. He'll know what to do with it. I also have some dictation." His secretary took the papers and put her pen to the steno pad. "Martha, this is Alaina Johansson. Alaina, this is my personal secretary, Martha."

Martha turned to Alaina and politely said, "Pleased to meet you," and turned back toward Alexander, ready for his dictation.

Alaina guessed she was about forty and shorter than most Americans she had seen. There was no ring to signify marriage and as she started taking down a letter, Alaina noticed she was very efficient in her job, no doubt the reason she was his personal secretary and not one of the others she had noticed looking out of their offices, trying to make eye contact with Alexander.

As they worked, Alaina got up and walked around the immense office. Windows covered one entire wall allowing a spectacular view of Manhattan. The setting sun spilled the last of its red rays, giving the room an uncharacteristically warm feeling. On the remaining walls, which were covered with silver wallpaper, hung various paintings from several different artists, some quite dated, others apparently modern art. The silver-blue carpet contrasted with the furnishings that were early American cherry wood antiques.

In a niche along the wall directly behind her stood a large coat of mail, larger than what she thought could be real, but looking incredibly authentic. As she looked at the wall above the niche, she saw a shield bearing a coat of arms along with a large jeweled sword that she estimated was from fifteenth century England. Hesitantly, she reached out to it, almost afraid to touch it. She had read so many stories about the Knights of the Round

Table and other knight stories, that she almost expected it to come alive before her.

Alexander frowned as he continued to watch her instead of concentrating on his dictation. He had seen her hesitate to touch the mail, and now watched how her slender fingers timidly explored it. He had the insane notion that he wanted to trade places with the mail, to feel her fingers exploring his body. "Thanks, Martha. Enough for now."

Alexander stood up and moved around his desk to stand behind her.

"Where did you get this?" Alaina asked with admiration.

"It's a family heirloom," he stated. As she looked at him pleading for more, he continued, "It's been in the family since the fourteenth century."

"English?" she asked.

"Scottish."

"It's beautiful!"

She felt she should give attention to the other objects in the room and walked to the nearest picture.

"Do you like that one?" he asked, grinning.

She looked at the painting that made no sense to her at all and said, "It's interesting."

"At best," he laughed, "but I bought it three years ago for $150,000 and it's tripled in value since. It's just an investment, you won't hurt my feelings."

She continued around the room until she stood in front of one of the windows and watched as the lights began to light the darkening city. She felt his arm come around her, pulling her up against his body.

"It has its own beauty," he stated as he stood still behind her, holding her. She felt that tight feeling in her abdomen that she felt every time she was this close to Alexander. "I'd like to take you to the theater tonight," Alexander said softly into her silky hair. "I thought you might enjoy Disney's *Beauty and the Beast.*"

Alaina pulled away from him and met no resistance. She walked over to his desk and turned to face him, feeling safer with a few yards between them. "I've heard about the theater and always wished to see one. But I thought you would show me the rest of Devon Maxwell's company."

He smiled at her, making no effort to move closer to her, instead, he leaned against the glass of the window with his arms folded, contemplating her. "We will have lots of time for that tomorrow. I'm expecting you to start work tomorrow on my committee to build the next ski resort for the rich and famous, making Maxwell Enterprises even richer."

She felt more at ease knowing now that she would have something to do starting tomorrow. She relaxed and flashed Alexander a big smile. "In that case, I would love to go."

He laughed, and his rich baritone voice sent small sensations through her soul. "We'll have to change into something more formal," he said, heading for the door adjoining his office.

She followed him into what he called the board room, which was filled with chairs, a long table and a bar at one end. There were also mirrors on all sides of the room, and a large chandelier hanging in the center. This room was done entirely in black and gold, and as she stood in awe of the elegance of it all, Alexander opened a few of the mirrors, exposing an enormous closet filled with suits, and to her surprise, the clothing she had been fitted for in Italy.

"As soon as they were finished, Sofia sent them air freight to my office. As you can see I keep quite a few clothes here. It seems I live here more than at my penthouse." He looked at the satin dress she had her fingers on and nodded his approval. "There's a powder room over there." He pointed to a door at the other end of the room. "You can change in there if you like."

She walked through a beautifully engraved glass door and entered another enormous room, again very elegantly and tastefully appointed. She wondered if all of this had been done to Alexander's taste. She quickly dressed and noticed to her great embarrassment that the dress fit her as tightly as her matching gloves, showing off every curve in detail and exposing much of her back. She stood looking in the mirror for quite some time, afraid to go out and tell Alexander that she could not wear this dress anywhere. After quite some time, she heard a soft knock on the door.

"Do you need help with a zipper or something?" he asked kindly. When he didn't receive an answer, he added, "I can get my secretary, if you like."

Alaina thought for a moment and finally opened the door a crack and said, "I think that might be a good idea, I don't think the dress fits quite right."

A few minutes later a knock came again and a firm voice asked, "Miss Johansson, may I come in?"

Alaina opened the door at once. "It's too small," Alaina gasped. "I can't go anywhere like this!"

"You look beautiful," Martha answered emotionlessly, although that seemed to be her normal tone of voice. "Someone with a figure like yours can wear anything. Unfortunately there are many more with less of a figure who do." She walked around her, appraising her. "Would you like me to fix your hair?"

Alaina readily accepted her help. She watched as Martha took out a brush and some pins from a drawer and started brushing her hair. Alaina closed her eyes as she felt the brush glide through her hair and she thought of her mother.

She saw Martha watching her in the mirror and realized she had seen her sadness. Martha smiled for the first time as if to console her. "There, that's perfect."

"You're very kind," Alaina said.

"Not usually," Martha admitted flatly.

"I don't believe that one minute," Alaina insisted. "I can see it in your eyes."

They heard a knock at the door again, and Martha went to open it, but Alaina stopped her for a moment. "May I call you Martha?" Martha nodded and Alaina asked softly, "I don't know anyone besides Alexander in this country, and I would like it very much if...we could be friends?"

"Why not? I'm not a great one for friends, but when in need...." Martha opened the door then and allowed Alaina to exit first. Alexander had stepped to the other side of the room, and stood behind the bar. As he saw her appear, his drink stopped in midair.

Alaina watched as he put the drink down and came around the bar, the glamour of his sudden, lazy grin making her pulse quicken. As he came to stand before her, she saw the enthralling fervor in his expression and felt something deep within her respond. "You look incredible," he finally said, his voice husky.

"Martha helped me," she said, trying to ignore her reaction to his closeness. Her skin shivered, yet she felt incredibly hot at the same time.

"I'll be leaving for the day if you don't need me," Martha said.

He nodded, his gaze never leaving Alaina, and said, "We'll have to hurry or we'll be late."

Filled with excitement, she watched the crowds as the limousine pulled onto Broadway and arrived at the Palace Theatre. She followed

Alexander through the crowd, holding on to his hand tightly. People wanted to stop him and talk to him, but Alexander seemed oblivious to their reaction as he continued walking, nodding at some, briefly shaking hands with others, until finally they were seated.

"Don't be offended I didn't introduce you now, I will during intermission," he explained. "They're about to begin and I wanted you to enjoy it from beginning to end."

She wanted to comment on how many people knew him, but before she could, she heard the orchestra tuning their instruments, and then the magic started.

Alexander watched her as much as he watched the program, enjoying the array of emotions that washed over her face one by one. He saw tears appear on a few occasions and a smile shyly appear on her lips every time she looked over and caught him watching her. He had known she would love this, as he knew she would love running horses over the meadows on the ranch in Wyoming. There was such a refreshing spontaneity about her, something he hadn't felt in a very long time. She was so different from the women he had seen in the past, who were after his money or his prestige. He had become some sort of trophy to some, but it hadn't mattered to him.

Not until now.

Intermission was upon them before Alexander was ready to share her with those business associates that had been staring at them during the program.

Alexander introduced her to the people next to them, and they stepped into the corridor. There were many admiring glances from men, and many hostile stares and comments from a few of the women he knew. Making sure Alaina was in hearing distance, one of the woman closest to them said to another, "This must be the latest paramour in his collection."

"I hear she's from some Arab country," another said.

Alexander saw her pale. "Would you like to go back to our seats?"

She nodded. Here were women that looked similar to herself and yet she was still made to feel the outcast. Tears welled in her eyes, and she bit her lip in concentration, not wanting a single tear to fall.

She felt anger building in Alexander. "Damn them all," he said quietly. "Let's get out of here."

Alexander took her back to his penthouse and outside on to the patio. She found herself surrounded by a lush garden and absolute quiet, except for the sound of a fountain trickling water down the side of a mermaid's tail. She heard Alexander's footsteps and turned to see him coming with a drink for her. "What do you think?"

"It's beautiful up here. Now I understand how people in the city can stay here. But not everyone in these buildings has a place like this, do they?"

He smiled at her question. "No, they don't. Unfortunately, money is the answer even to this."

She took the drink from him and grimaced. "What is this?"

"Soda."

"It's very sweet."

"People like it for that reason. Would you like my wine instead?"

"No, thank you." She turned and looked into the large room off the patio. "Why do you have a separate elevator up to this garden?"

"Security."

"It seems this is a much more dangerous place than where I come from. People have bodyguards and secret elevators—it's not at all what I expected." She turned to him again, finding him closer than before. "Are all places in America like this?"

"No. On the ranch in Wyoming everyone is safe, except for the occasional wild animal that feasts upon people."

Alaina caught the smile in his eyes. "Wild animals are not as dangerous as people can be. Animals are usually predictable. Most of the people I met tonight...I couldn't guess what they might do or say."

"I predict you will learn that quickly." Alexander put his drink down and took her by the hand, leading her towards the patio doors, having seen her look in that direction numerous time. "Would you like a tour of the place?"

"Yes, very much."

Alaina was not disappointed. It was filled with archaeological finds from all over the world and priceless works of art.

"Is this a dinosaur bone?" she asked, feeling how rough the exterior was.

"Yes, when I was little I loved dinosaurs, especially the T-Rex."

She tried to picture him as a little boy, but it was hard to imagine that he was ever anything but the powerful man that seemed to fill the room with his presence. "Where did you get all these wonderful things?"

"I've traveled and collected," he said while rearranging the wood in the fireplace. He sat down on the couch and waited for her to sit down beside him.

Alaina could feel he was watching her again. "What are you thinking about?"

"That I should get you home so you can put in a full day's work tomorrow. Maxwell Enterprises opens for business at seven thirty."

She sank back in the couch, "I like your home."

He smiled. "What's wrong? Change your mind about working for me? Did people tip you off tonight what a tyrant I am to work for?"

Alaina understood now when he was teasing, but she felt sad. "Where is home for me, Alexander?"

As he watched her look ever more lost, he gave in to the urge of pulling her close. He buried his face in her glorious soft hair, surprising himself at the tenderness he felt for her, touched that she was so honest with her emotions. As he felt her arm rest on his chest and her head sink on his heart, other thoughts beyond tenderness entered his mind and he felt his body reacting to her again. He whispered, "Ubi bene ibi patria," into her hair.

*Home is where your heart is,* Alaina translated silently. "But I don't even know where my heart is anymore." Yet, deep down, she knew she was home. Her heart belonged to Alexander.

But she still had to keep her obligation to her mother and see if Devon Maxwell would take her as his bride. She could not let the feelings surface, yet keeping them inside brought a sharp pain into her heart and she abruptly stood up. "I wish I could be free of this engagement to Devon Maxwell," she blurted out.

Alexander was quiet for a moment. "Why don't you just explain that to him? I'm sure he'll be calling you this week."

Alaina immediately felt remorse for her disloyalty. "I'm sorry. I shouldn't have said that."

"I understand." There was no trace of emotion in Alexander's tone.

# Chapter 11

The next morning Alexander's limousine picked her up from the Plaza and dropped her off at Maxwell Enterprises. It was not yet seven in the morning, and yet the office building was already alive with workers. Alaina immediately went to see Martha, who was on the phone when she approached.

She greeted her and held up one finger for her to wait one minute. While she had a moment, she said, "Alexander wanted me to put you on the company insurance plan right away and I have filled out all the forms as much as I could. You might want to look over the paperwork and then sign here on this line."

While Martha was on the phone, Alaina looked over the information and signed it. *So now I had health insurance*, she thought.

The rest of the day Martha gave her a tour of the fifteen floors and an overview of what Maxwell Enterprises did through its New York headquarters. "Maxwell Enterprises owns many companies all around the country and some in foreign countries. Many retain their original names and employees while others are totally stripped of everything including their names and sold off. This is where a team of analysts investigates new merger possibilities or acquisitions and then brings their ideas to Alexander. And there is where all the bean-counters sit."

"Bean-counters?"

"Finances."

"So Alexander makes all the decisions for Maxwell Enterprises?"

"He has signing power. He's the president."

"What does Devon Maxwell do?"

"Collects the money," Martha's mouth tightened. "But that's all I really can say about him."

"You don't like Devon Maxwell?"

"I've never met the man. I really couldn't say."

Alaina persisted. She had to find out something about the man who she was to marry, and Alexander hadn't told her much. "But you don't like him?"

They had returned to Martha's desk. "Why are you interested?"

"I'm to marry him."

Martha blinked several times rapidly as if she had a speck in her eye and then recovered from her shock. "Is that why Alexander brought you here? Is Devon Maxwell going to finally put in an appearance after all these years?" She sounded as if she couldn't breathe. "Excuse me. I need to go to the ladies room."

Alaina watched her walk away briskly. A voice came over a box on her desk. "Martha, can you come in, please?"

It was Alexander. She didn't know how to tell him Martha wasn't there and didn't want to push a wrong button, so she went to the door of his office and opened it slowly.

Alexander was on the phone and as he saw her, he summoned her in. He didn't smile a greeting to her this morning and his eyes were an icy blue. He hung up and asked, "Was the room to your satisfaction?"

"Yes, thank you," she replied. "It's a beautiful hotel."

"I have to return to Italy on business this afternoon. I trust Martha is taking care of your needs."

She winced at the coldness in his tone and wondered what she had done to make him treat her this way. Could it be the comment about wishing to be free from Devon Maxwell that made him react this way?

"Yes, she's very sweet."

His mouth curved on one side. It was the first sliver of warmth Alaina had seen on his hard, set face. "I've never heard anyone comment about Martha in quite that way before. Is there anything I can do for you before I leave?"

"Tell me when you'll return." She didn't want them parting with the feeling there was something wrong between them.

"I'm sorry. I never know these things for sure. Business is not always predictable."

She was losing the battle without even knowing what had started it. "Will Devon Maxwell call today?"

"Why don't we call him? You can use my office, which will afford you total privacy." He got up and pulled his chair out for her to sit down.

She swallowed hard and then convinced herself that maybe now she could straighten out her life and know better which way her future would go. Alexander dialed a long sequence of numbers and handed the phone to Alaina.

With her heart suddenly pounding and her face feeling warm, she heard on the other end of the phone someone answer, "Meadow Creek Ranch."

"Yes, hello. My name is Alaina Johansson and I would like to speak to Mr. Devon Maxwell, please." She was so nervous about speaking to Devon Maxwell, she didn't realize when Alexander left.

He had gone without saying good-bye.

"Just one moment, please," the answer came.

Alaina noticed her fingers were shaking and she fought for calm.

The same voice answered again, "He's indisposed at the moment. Can he return the call in a few minutes?"

"Hello?" a voice interrupted the line.

"Here he is," the first voice said. "He's picked up on his line. An Alaina Johansson is on the line to speak with you." Then she heard a clicking sound on the line.

"Miss Johansson, how nice of you to call."

She wanted to cry. What could she say to this man her mother had made arrangements for her to marry, when her heart belonged to another man? "I hope I haven't interrupted you..."

"No, not at all. I'm afraid we're both in a rather awkward position, and I apologize."

At least he wasn't unpleasant on the phone. "Mr. Maxwell, I need to ask you something up front that is very important to me."

"Yes?"

Tears rolled down Alaina's checks now. It was hard to talk because it felt as if a peach pit was stuck in her throat.

"Why didn't you come for me yourself?"

There, it was out. Maybe if he would have come for her, she would have fallen in love with him just as she had many years ago and she wouldn't be in this dilemma now.

There was silence on the line for a moment.

Then with what seemed genuine concern in his voice, he asked, "Was Alexander not agreeable to you? Did he hurt you in any way?"

"No," she answered. She immediately felt she had to defend Alexander, fearing she had put wrong thoughts into Devon's head. "He was... fine." She couldn't think of a suitable word.

"Fine? Are you all right, Miss Johansson?"

She wanted to shout *no*, but she dried her tears with her hand and asked what she had to know. "Mr. Maxwell, are you planning on accepting my mother's request for this marriage between the families?"

"How do feel about the request?"

"Well, we've never met, and...."

"Yes, and I apologize again. Things are crazy around the ranch right now. When you come out, I'd like to be able to spend some time with you, so why don't you fly out next month, say on the sixteenth. Is that acceptable?"

*Oh dear*, the conversation was not going the way she had intended. Maybe it wouldn't hurt to get to know him again. It would be more polite to tell him that she was in love with someone else in person. "Yes, that will be fine. And thank you for your generosity. I would like to explain that I am not penniless and would like to pay for my own expenses."

"Why, you dishonor me, Alaina. Your grandfather and my grandfather have always extended hospitalities to one another. I must insist that when you are in this country, I will take care of your needs."

She knew she couldn't win. "Thank you."

"We'll see you soon, then."

The phone line went dead and that was the end of their conversation. She felt like screaming.

She did not want him taking care of her needs!

She sat in the chair for quite some time, staring out the windows until Martha entered the office many hopeless thoughts later.

"Alaina, I'm leaving for the day. I have some personal business. Can I be of assistance before I leave?"

"Martha, who is Devon Maxwell?"

"I don't know the man."

"Then Alexander. Tell me about him."

"I'd rather you talked with him, if you have any questions."

"Please...."

Martha sat down in the chair before her. "I guess there is no harm in telling you things you will find out eventually anyway, from either hearsay or speculation. There are many things I don't know, but only guess. I've been his employee for ten years now and hardly know him any better than the day I walked into his office and applied for the job of executive secretary. Circumstances have changed tremendously, but he has remained the same man."

Alaina noticed she sat so straight in the chair she was worried her back would snap. She knew immediately Martha was uncomfortable talking about Alexander. Maybe if they weren't in his office. "Martha, would you have lunch with me? That is, if you don't have other plans."

"I was going to grab something on the way."

"Good, it's settled then."

"I know a nice diner that's quaint, just around the corner, where I sometimes get lunch. We could walk."

"Let's go," Alaina said, feeling much better.

During lunch Alaina learned no more about Martha than she already knew. She was very adept at avoiding issues and getting Alaina to talk about herself. "It's your turn," Alaina said finally over coffee. "I think you know almost everything about me, but I know nothing about you, except that you live with your cat."

"There's not much to say really. I'm not married...."

"Have you ever been in love?"

Alaina saw a flash of pain in her light brown eyes and, instantly, she was sorry she had asked. "Please don't think about it, if it causes you pain."

"No, I've held it in a long time. That's probably why the pain is still there. One day I must deal with it, but it's hard when one has harbored pain for so many years. But I wanted to tell you about Alexander before you heard gossip."

Alaina noticed immediately she had diverted the subject away from herself again, but it didn't matter now. She was going to talk about her beloved Alexander.

"I really don't know that much about him. As I'm sure you've discovered, he's a very private man." She sipped her coffee.

"Tell me when you first met him. That was ten years ago. How old was he?"

"I believe around twenty-two and sharp as they come. He was a nobody in New York back then. He had less than one hundred thousand dollars to work with and could only pay me twenty-five thousand a year. I would have laughed had I not seen the hunger and determination in him. He explained he couldn't pay me any more right away, but promised as he earned more, I would also earn more. I was thirty-seven and accustomed to twice as much money."

"So why did you take the job?"

She smiled slightly. "There were at least ten other girls waiting for an interview who had passed his criteria. They were all younger than I was and dressed smartly. You see, Alexander's picture had appeared in the *New York Times* the week before. Need I say more? They were all snickering and whispering about my dress and my age, that he would never hire anyone as old as me."

"You obviously showed them."

"It was more than that. It was Alexander himself. I had heard that Maxwell Enterprises had gone under because Alexander's uncle had stripped the company and skipped the country, leaving his only son, Devon, and Devon's cousin, Alexander, penniless. It was a company built up by their grandfather and inherited solely by his daughter, Devon's mother. I wondered in the beginning why Alexander, who stood much less to gain than Devon, came to New York, but then I remembered reading about a fire at the ranch in Wyoming and it was suggested that Devon Maxwell had been seriously burned in the fire. So Devon had the money and Alexander had the looks. And he definitely has the Midas touch. He's turned that original hundred thousand and multiplied it exponentially."

Alaina sat back against the chair. They were sitting in the far corner, away from anyone else, fearing someone would overhear their quiet conversation. Alaina tried to breathe, tried to focus on the person closest to them, but couldn't. Devon and Alexander were cousins! One was wealthy and scarred; one was worldly and beautiful. Two contrasts, yet she had loved both of them in her young life.

What else could there be in Alexander's life that he couldn't share with her? She smiled at Martha. She had a plan now. She would show both of them that she could take care of herself and then Devon wouldn't feel obligated to marry her and she could win Alexander's love. She would somehow heal the hurt he'd suffered in his past, and Alexander could turn her money into much more money and start his own company, if he wanted to.

"Martha, if you had two million dollars, what would you do with it?"

Martha saw Alaina was serious and answered very professionally, "Give it to Alexander."

"I can't."

"I don't know, then. There are many investment possibilities."

"You must have a pretty good idea, being his secretary, what is profitable."

"I think I understand what you're asking. I could show you more in detail what Alexander is working on, but I can't be disloyal to Alexander. He pays me a lot of money to keep my mouth shut, among other things."

"I would never want you to do anything disloyal, Martha. I only want to know where to invest my money on my own. It's time I get out on my own. And I also need an apartment. Can you help me with that?"

"I know a real-estate agent who's very good. She knows the best leases in the area. It's going to cost you to live anywhere around Wall Street."

"Where do you live?"

"Brooklyn, but I don't know if you'd like it."

"What about right across the water from Wall Street?"

"Brooklyn Heights? There are some nice brownstones and it is very clean. You might find something there. Ask the real estate agent. I'll get you her card."

"Martha, please say nothing to Alexander about any of this, all right?"

"I'm good at saying nothing to no one." Martha smiled at her own joke.

Alaina's happiness soared now that she had a plan and it seemed she was taking control of her own life. She took Martha's hand and squeezed it. "Thank you."

"I haven't done anything."

"You're my friend. That means a lot to me. Will you have time tomorrow to help me?"

"Alexander is gone and he has actually given me a light load and asked me to help you with anything you need."

"You see. You even have his permission."

Martha smiled. "I don't think that's quite what he had in mind."

The next morning Martha brought in some charts of the company and its different branches into Alexander's office.

"Why are we in Alexander's office?" Alaina asked.

"It's soundproof and no one would dare enter without knocking. We have total privacy."

"Martha, I understand Alexander is very smart, but there are many smart people in the world. Why has Alexander succeeded where others haven't?"

Martha stirred her coffee and answered thoughtfully. "He's very thorough, yet he looks for the big picture. There are different patterns and systems, he explained to me once. If I say he senses the gestalt in the world around him, do you understand what I mean?"

"I think so."

"He used to do the analyzing, designing and decision-making all alone, in the beginning. Now he has teams of specialists for all of that and he is left with the final decisions."

"But he travels a lot, doesn't he?"

"He is still the person people trust in different countries and that's what makes the international branch of the company so successful. Many will only deal with him, not the company. They trust him, and have a relationship with him. Recently, Alexander created a team of professionals he takes along with him, after they've lived in the country for a while. They get a feel for the culture and customs in the country that way."

"Alexander must have lived in my country before. He fit in perfectly in the desert. I thought he was a Bedouin at first."

"I typed a memo to one of our newer employees who is to travel with Alexander to Saudi next spring. Let me see if I can find it." She went to a file drawer and pulled out a manila folder. It was filled with newspaper clippings and several memos. "You can read it."

There was a background memo Alaina found interesting. She read the first page of the two-page memo and she nodded, commenting to Martha. "It's all true. Bedouins are often powerful and have the authority and financial resources. They also preserve the old customs. Is that who he deals with mostly?" she asked, surprised.

Martha smiled. "Keep reading."

The memo next spoke about the Arab elite, who were either born into royalty or the middle class who had reached the top echelons of industry or government. "Is this true? It says that most of these, who at home wear the traditional robes, offer floor cushions and shun alcohol, in the West act in western ways?"

"I'll introduce you to some gentlemen next time we have a meeting in New York. You won't be able to tell the difference in dress or habits." Martha seemed to be enjoying herself for some reason.

"Well, the rest of the things, like our weekend

being Thursday and Friday, or Friday being our day of rest, is all correct."

"Our?" Martha asked.

Alaina smiled shyly. "Habit."

Martha pointed to some notes. "Did you know about this?"

"Inshallah. It means 'God is willing.' Arabs believe God's will determines what gets done, no matter how sincere a person's intentions."

"It makes scheduling incredible frustrating."

Alaina continued to read and started laughing softly. "He knew all along," she said.

"What?"

"He writes here that even mild American expletives are shocking." She saw Martha was watching her closely. She felt a blush creep into her cheeks and she shook her head. "Never mind."

She scanned the next items and asked, "Aren't some of these other things just common courtesy in this country also, such as not criticizing or raising your voice in public, turning your back on someone or pointing your finger at them? This one I don't understand, why would you pat anyone on the back or call him a friend, if he really isn't?"

"Americans are just different. We consider everyone a friend until they've made themselves our enemy."

Alexander obviously knew the rules and when to break them. She realized that Mustafa and Alexander had been trading insults in the desert.

The rest of the memo was just more on behavior when visiting, such as blowing your nose in public being the height of vulgarity and not walking in front of someone praying; followed by more Arab values. One caught her attention, one of the most important: family honor.

Those two words brought back the image of

her mother, Zainab, and immediately her conscience troubled her. Her mother would have expected her to honor her wishes of marriage.

She put the memo down. She'd think about it later.

"Does he have more papers such as these?"

"It's quite interesting, isn't it?" She returned the folder and searched through more folders. "I remember writing a memo once to a female executive that was accompanying a team to South America. She wasn't married or engaged and Alexander suggested she either borrow an engagement ring or he would provide one on loan. A big diamond engagement ring." Martha smiled.

"Why not a wedding ring?" Alaina asked.

"Well, if you think about it, a large stone tells other men that your finance is wealthy, right? And an engagement ring tell them you're still in love. Two serious setbacks for most men in most countries."

Alaina giggled. "Maybe I should buy myself an engagement ring before Alexander offers to give me one on loan," she said. *I want one from him that I can keep*, she thought.

"I enjoyed writing a memo to an executive who had just been asked to move to London and acclimate before doing business there, but I can't seem to find it."

"Aren't the United States and England very similar?"

"That's where so many businessmen make mistakes. And that's where Alexander has an upper hand. You see, Europeans watch us more than the other way around. What Americans may view as strictly domestic has sometimes weighty consequences for Europeans. But then again, mostly I believe it's because Alexander is extremely observant."

"And he can blend in and observe and listen before he acts," Alaina added, remembering the very first time she saw him.

"Do you know anything about World War II?" Martha asked.

"I had quite extensive history lessons from my tutor."

"Then you understand the Marshall Plan?"

"Yes, I think so."

"Well, not only have many never forgiven the U.S. for entering the war when it felt like it, which they feel was very late, and then winning it for them, but many thought the Marshall Plan was a scheme to force them to import American goods."

"So there's not much trust, even though they've been allies?"

"You have to earn their trust."

"And Alexander has built up that trust?"

"Yes, and that's one of the reasons he's so successful."

"But I can't build up that kind of trust instantly."

"Right, so what you need to do is invest within the United States. Here people are aggressive and are accustomed to instant results."

Alaina thought about it for a moment. "I can understand that, but I don't know many Americans yet, so I don't know what they are like."

"You'll find out soon enough. In the meantime, here's some information you might find useful." Martha handed her some more files.

# Chapter 12

The days went by quickly and Alaina absorbed everything Martha could tell her about Alexander and about the company. She learned much about running a business, but the more she learned, the more confused she became about where to invest her money.

Alexander returned at the end of the week and as confusing as her situation at work was to her, her private life became quickly more perplexing. Upon Alexander's return, he showed her the town, introduced her to many interesting and influential people, took her to exclusive restaurants, dancing at exciting night clubs, and yet, it was the quiet moments in the limousine and the quiet walks to her hotel room that were the most exciting. She always felt he would kiss her and hold her, yet he never touched her. Sometimes when they were alone, she could see passion in his gaze, yet it would cloud up and disappear as soon as someone walked by or interrupted them. He never spoke of the future, and she was afraid to ask about it.

She tried not to think about her engagement to Devon Maxwell, yet it was always there between them. She could not allow herself to forget it. She told herself she had to hear an answer from him before she could allow herself to love Alexander. But her heart knew differently.

One night as Alexander was working late, Alaina came up to his office, wanting just to watch him work, and to occasionally look out the window at the many lights over Manhattan. Nighttime was Alaina's favorite time in the city, when all the dirt and grime disappeared in the darkness, and the lights allowed the illusion of serenity.

Alexander was busy with paper work and hardly noticed her presence until she started fogging up the windows with her excitement and tried to clear it with a swipe of her hand. "What is it?" he asked, curious now. Alexander got up and stood next to her. "It's snowing."

"What does it feel like? It never snowed when we were skiing."

"How would you like to go ice-skating?" Alexander asked.

"Is it like skiing?"

"Sort of," he replied, watching her.

"Now?"

"Now. Go get your coat," he said and laughed out loud as he watched her run down the hall. He called Joe and they drove to Madison Square Garden where they laced up and headed onto the ice.

Joe skated by them and mumbled to Alexander, "The older ones are easier on my bones, boss."

"You're the one who insisted on skating with us," Alexander answered, smiling.

"I'm trying to do my job, boss."

Alaina let go of Alexander's hand and skated faster, yelling, "This is great!" But she hadn't figured out how to stop yet.

"Are you gonna be needin' me later? I need to soak my tired muscles."

"No, I thought I'd make our skating star some hot chocolate at my place," Alexander said watching Alaina.

"I've seen that look before, boss. I'll stay out of your way, then."

Alexander was going to answer Joe, when Alaina fell down, sprawling on the ice. Both men were by her side in seconds only to see her laughing too hard to stand up again. "Winter is wonderful!" she shouted.

"Only if you don't have to drive in it," Joe muttered and grabbed Alaina's arm to help her up.

"You ready to call it quits?" Alexander asked hopefully.

It was Alaina's turn to laugh at him. "All right, I am getting a little cold."

Joe watched through the rear view mirror of the open cab and shook his head. Alexander was laughing with Alaina as she pulled at him to stand up through the limousine's sunroof. She opened her mouth to catch snow flakes on her tongue. "You have to try this," she said. "Come on," she encouraged. Gradually, her coercion convinced him to enjoy the childish whim, and Alaina loved the sound of his laughter.

They dropped back into the seat as Joe parked the limousine and left to go to his own adjoining apartment. Alexander and Alaina went to make hot chocolate and then Alaina curled up next to Alexander on the couch in front of the crackling fire.

"Alexander, can I ask you a personal question?"

"You may ask."

"Do you believe in God?" she asked slowly.

Alexander was totally caught off guard. He hadn't been asked that in a very long time, and then only by his mother, never by a woman in his arms—they usually had very different questions. "Which one?"

"The God in Heaven, of the Universe. Is there any other?"

"Some people call the dollar almighty. Then there are superstars...."

"You're avoiding the question."

Alexander was quiet for a moment. "Yes."

Alaina smiled happily. "So do I. I'm glad you do. I had a tutor once, for Latin, and we studied many writings, including the *Bible.* We also studied the Greek philosophies, but I was partial to the tragedies."

"Now there's a subject I'm better versed in," Alexander said, relaxing completely and stretching one leg out on the couch while keeping the other bent at the knee, as he pulled her in between his legs with her back cradled on his chest.

They spent the next several hours telling stories until Alaina's eyes became heavy and Alexander carried her to his guest room. She was asleep before he laid her down, and he sat next to her, watching her sleep, wondering what it would be like to wake up with her in the morning. *Such a trusting soul,* he thought, forcing himself away and going to his desk. He still had work to do.

The next morning Alexander called Joe and asked if he wanted breakfast. "Alaina's in the shower. How do you want your eggs?" Alexander enjoyed cooking breakfast.

"The usual. So how was your evening, boss?"

"I told Alaina stories and she fell asleep on me."

"Excuse me if I say so, but that sounds unusual for you, boss, knowing how the ladies like you. Sounds sort of boring."

"Refreshing, actually." Alexander felt better than he had in years. If they had made love, perhaps he would have felt even better. But the crazy thing was, he felt good just being with her.

Later that afternoon, Alexander called Alaina into his office. "I have to leave on business again. I'd like you to consider staying at the penthouse while I'm gone."

She started to refuse but he insisted on it, convincing her it was safer than the hotel. She had an appointment with the real-estate agent the next day and decided she wouldn't be ready to move quite yet anyway.

"I've also hired a bodyguard for you. Joe is coming with me on this trip."

She didn't care about the bodyguard and she didn't want him to go again. "How long will you be gone?" She couldn't bear looking at him as she asked; she was already missing him.

He walked from around his desk and pulled her chin up to meet her eyes. "Will you miss me?" She nodded. "One, maybe two weeks. I'll try to hurry home." A smile came to his lips, "I've never considered anywhere home," he said softly, "but you've changed that somehow."

Alaina instinctively knew that this was a big moment for him, for he was opening up to her. She wanted to tell him she loved him, but the words wouldn't come out. They stood in silence for a moment and then Alexander reached for his jacket. "The plane's waiting," he said, escorting her to the door. "Work hard and make us rich." He chuckled softly and kissed her quickly on the lips as he left.

The only thing Alaina remembered was *us*.

Before Alaina left Maxwell Enterprises that evening, Martha introduced her to her bodyguard. Mike was younger than Joe and somewhat bigger all the way around. Alaina immediately felt uncomfortable around him, especially the way he kept smiling at her.

"Excuse me," Alaina said to Mike, and took Martha aside for a moment. "Did Alexander hire him for me?"

"He is new and I know he came with the highest qualifications and references. He flew in from Washington today," Martha explained. "If you don't like him, I'm sure Alexander will hire someone else."

"No, it's fine," Alaina immediately countered, not wanting to be a problem. "He's just so different from Joe. I guess I expected someone like him, someone more distant." She put her coat on and smiled at Martha. "I'll see you in the morning."

Martha nodded, looking at her watch. "Six thirty already, I'll be awhile. Are you attending the McCalls' dinner tonight?" Martha asked, handing her the invitation.

"I don't want to go alone."

"There's Mike," Martha said, leaning her head in his direction.

Alaina looked over to Mike, who was in conversation with the long legged blond secretary down the hall. Alaina sighed, shaking her head. "No, I think I'll try to make myself at home in Alexander's place. I'll be staying there until Alexander gets back."

Martha nodded. "You'll find your things already at his place. He had me call the hotel earlier."

Alaina arrived at the penthouse shortly after seven, escorted by Mike, and found her things neatly inside the front door. She found a note from the cleaning woman that she had signed for the suitcases inside the apartment. *How efficient everything is in Alexander's world*, Alaina thought. Did he have such power over all the people he dealt with? Was he so used to having his way? Alaina shrugged off her questions and got busy carrying her suitcases into the guest bedroom. She knew

Mike was across the hall, ready to help her, but she preferred the solitude.

After she unpacked and had a shower, she decided to roam the penthouse, everywhere except Alexander's bedroom. She couldn't bring herself to enter his private room for he was such a private person, and she felt as if she would be intruding. There was plenty to look at and read in the other rooms he had shown her earlier.

To her delight, in the library she found over a thousand books, all categorized and numbered. She gasped at some of the titles and smiled at others, such as *One Thousand and One Arabian Nights*. She found a section of business books and decided she'd broaden her mind in this way, and on the same shelf, strangely enough, she also found several spy/action novels. It was very strange, since everything else was categorized and in order. She took several out and discovered they were written by the same author and signed the same way in each book: *To my favorite spy.*

She brought those along with the business books into the living room and curled up in front of the fireplace, reading and learning about economics, the banking system, and high corporate financing. One book she read about banking was signed by Douglas McClyde, Alexander's grandfather, who she later read was one of the founders of the Federal Reserve Commission.

Again, she wondered about Alexander's life and why his aunt had inherited all the family wealth when there were other grandchildren. His life must have been hard growing up. Was that why he had learned to adapt to different environments as well as he did? One day she would find out, she promised herself.

Then she started reading one of the spy novels and read long into the night, unable to put it down.

She read one entire book every night for the next three nights. The spy's nickname was Lucky, and she learned that he always managed to escape the situation that had built into sheer suspense with seemingly all odds against him, and he always ended up with the girl.

Alexander found himself back in the desert. "It's time we make a decision," he said to Ziegler.

Ziegler, the CIA agent in charge, shook his head. "We haven't had time to make a qualified judgment call."

"I agree with Alexander," Skalski said. "He knows this country better than any of us." Skalski had been with the CIA for most of his life and rarely gambled. He dealt with solid facts, and Alexander accepted the faith that had been placed in his judgment.

"I can't accept the odds. It's too hit-or-miss." Ziegler did not retreat.

"We ignore the odds." Alexander spoke quietly. The other two men listened. "There are people being held hostage in that home that happen to be my friends. This is personal. We split up. You two enter from the roof and I'll enter from the rear. If we delay they might die, if they're not dead already. It's not Mustafa's style to release hostages, but he has surprised me by attacking such an influential family."

"There is no evidence that it is Mustafa," Skalski reminded Alexander.

"There is no doubt," Alexander said. "Cover me."

There was no firing from the home and everything looked deceptively normal. Alexander was able to make his way to the back of the house successfully. He signaled to the other two men with his .44 Magnum to head over to the house in the same way. He didn't wait for them to reach the roof before bursting through the back door, ready for any attack. Nothing could have prepared him for the shock as he stood staring in disbelief at the fragments of bodies around him.

Skalski and Ziegler entered the house and they, too, stood in shock, void of expression. "What happened?" Ziegler asked.

"I don't know," Alexander answered in a strained voice, foreign even to himself. He squatted down next to Abdul's body and lifted Abdul's head gently onto his leg. With his fingers he felt the bullet holes in his chest.

"I'm sorry, Alexander." Ziegler said softly. "We contacted you as soon as we found out what was going on. I owed you that much, but this...."

Alexander carefully laid his friend's body down on the ground and stood up. "Mustafa wasn't after the publicity—it was all too quiet. It could have been revenge, but more likely, it was money."

*Alaina*, he thought. *He's after the money. Alaina will inherit it all, and if he has Alaina....*

Alexander headed for the door without an explanation.

"Alexander, wait...."

Alexander couldn't wait for anyone. He knew their backup would arrive shortly and that Mustafa's men were far gone already. Alaina had to get to Wyoming, out of New York. She would be safer there, and Mustafa might hesitate if she was already married.

Alaina looked up from her book as she heard the apartment door open. Immediately she felt uneasy. Where was Mike? Who was coming in unannounced?

She stood up quietly and turned off the light

next to the couch. She waited for her eyes to adjust to the light change and pressed herself against the wall, hoping the intruder wouldn't notice her right away. The intruder wasn't being very quiet himself as he came through the kitchen.

As he came within her view, she saw a tall, slender man, perhaps in his late sixties, with very white hair that was slicked back and a thick long beard the same color. He turned on the light and she stepped forward to meet him. Dark blue, almost black eyes starred at her and she thought she detected humor there for a moment. "Who are you?" she asked.

"Well, now. I suppose I should ask you the same question, young lady." His voice had a distinct Scottish lilt to it.

"I'm Alaina Johansson. Alexander isn't here at the moment. Can I help you?"

"'Tarnation! So the young man was telling the truth." A look of anger crossed his face, but then he seemed to change. "Maybe all isn't lost. Tell me about yourself, lassie."

"First tell me who you are and how you got in here. Mike is...."

"Mike-Schmike. He's had a few too many drinks with me tonight to be any good to anyone. I told him what I'll tell you now. I'm Adam McClyde, related to the fella who is suppose to live here, but alas, if he wasn't about so much, I wouldn't get my facts for my stories."

"Stories?"

"I write books."

"What kind of books?" Alaina had never met a writer. She immediately decided she liked Adam McClyde.

"You know, spy kind-of stories. Now who did you say you were? Alexander usually doesn't allow anyone to stay at his place alone. You must be someone special." He smiled at her then.

"I'm to marry Devon Maxwell."

"Are you now? Alexander hasn't told you much then, has he? Always good with secrets, but I can always get him to talk." He had moved around to the mahogany wall unit and opened a panel which concealed several bottles of liqueur. "He still can't drink me under the table. He's been trying since he was barely old enough to drink, but never will."

Alaina noticed now the smell of scotch on his breath and wondered how much he had been drinking with Mike before he came to Alexander's apartment. "I like you now, and I'll let you in on a little secret if you promise not to tell him."

Alaina nodded watching him pour a large glass of scotch and downing it in one gulp. "I water my bottle down. Had to for many years now, otherwise I wouldn't be able to irritate him so." He paused before he added, "You won't tell and ruin one of an old man's few joys left in life, would you?"

Alaina laughed. "I wish I could best him in that way. Tell me more about your books."

He pointed to one of the books she had on the table. "*Shaded Sands*? You wrote that? That was my favorite! You're Richard Kingsley?"

"One and the same. Many authors have different pen names."

"This is wonderful. I love books, especially these. How do you write like that - where do you get your ideas?"

"I listen. Tell me about yourself."

Close to an hour had passed before Alaina noticed the time. She had told her story to this old man who, in some strange sense, she immediately felt close to, mostly because of the kindness he radiated. "Now tell me where you get the ideas for Lucky from?"

He drank another full glass down and then took his long arm and gestured around the room. "Many from this man and his travels. He's much like his grandfather. A true adventurer." He finished off the once-full bottle. "Blast that he's gone. I needed to talk to him and I flew all the way from Madrid yesterday."

"Madrid, Spain?"

He nodded.

"Mr. Kingsley, I mean McClyde...."

"Call me Adam. You're family now."

"Adam, how does Alexander give you ideas? From his business travels?"

Adam closed glassy-looking eyes for a moment and almost fell into the couch. "That's a cover for his activities with the CIA, and the CIA is a cover for his business. He has more names and identities in more countries...." He paused. "The poor lad, he was satisfied with his business ventures in the beginning, but when he didn't feel the excitement anymore, the rush of closing the deal, he got involved with...anyway—I write about him."

"Lucky is Alexander?"

"Well, I embellish some." Suddenly his eyes opened and he looked at her threateningly. "Now don't you ever call him that! He hates it—purely despises that nickname I gave him. He doesn't believe in luck—and don't you go and tell him I told you. I swore I'd never tell a soul. But since you're family now..." His eyes closed and he went limp from head to toe. For a moment Alaina wondered if he had fallen asleep.

Alaina sat quietly watching him and after a few minutes, whispered, "Mr. McClyde...Adam. Please, why don't you go sleep in Alexander's bedroom? I'm sure he won't mind."

His eyes lazily opened again and he seemed wide

awake. "No, I have a place to stay. Call a taxi for me, will you? Alex probably won't be back for a while. I'll catch him on my way back from California."

She called a taxi while he lay on the couch. She watched him sleep and wondered if Alexander would one day look like this man. The bell rang and Adam stood up. "There's my cab. Very nice meeting you, Alaina. I hope to see you again soon. Don't mention I stopped by, I like surprising Alexander, you know. He hates surprises."

She smiled and promised. She walked him to the door and watched him go down the hall. She closed the door and remembered the book on the table. She quickly went to the couch and picked up the book, reading it again. This time, she imagined Lucky was Alexander. It wasn't totally impossible, she reasoned. She had commented to Martha how well he fit into environments. But he was so business-like. Then she reminded herself of the man she had seen in the desert who had come to her rescue, and the man that had held a gun in his hand, ready to shoot men who were trying to kidnap her. There were definitely two sides to Alexander McClyde.

She found herself wanting to be the girl in the book that Lucky always got in the end.

Close to three a.m. she heard another person enter her room. She stayed where she was, curled up on the couch, and waited.

It was Mike. Alaina wondered if anything was wrong. "Can I help you?" she asked suspiciously, as she saw his tie hanging loosely around his neck and his eyes strangely glazed over.

"Well, I figured since the two of us have spent the last nights alone, maybe we should just share each other's loneliness."

"I'm not lonely," Alaina answered, trying to hide

the worry in her voice. She had seen that look in a man's eyes before and it frightened her. She got up and backed up as Mike came closer. "You've been drinking."

"An old man left me a bottle. Now come here and stop playing hard to get, eh? Or am I not good enough? Alexander McClyde has big money, but does he have what it takes here?" He patted his crotch.

"I think you've had too much to drink and if you leave now, I won't mention anything to Alexander..."

"Nothing is wrong, darling. And I'll prove it to you." He reached for her, but Alaina ducked away from him. She ran through Alexander's bedroom into the bathroom and locked the door.

She heard Mike laughing. "You can't stay in there forever. I'll be waiting."

Maybe if she acted calm and in control he would understand she just wasn't interested. "I'm going to take a long bath and I expect you to be gone when I'm finished," she shouted through the door, trying to sound commanding.

There wasn't an answer and she wondered if he had left. Just to be on the safe side, she decided to let the water run into the tub. When it was full, she listened at the door and heard sounds in the kitchen. She looked at the tub and decided a bath would soothe her nerves and maybe by the time she finished, he would be gone. She turned the whirlpool jets on and let the water massage her tight shoulder muscles. She started reading her novel again and it was just as suspenseful the second time around.

Several chapters later, she thought she heard strange sounds coming from Alexander's bedroom. She turned off the jets and heard a loud crash. She quickly gathered a towel around her and then stood by the door a few seconds trying to decide what to do. Finally, she opened the door slowly.

Alexander and Joe were there. "Alexander! I'm so happy to see you," she said, wanting to throw her arms around him, but with only a towel wrapped around her, modesty prevented her. Then she saw the bed was a terrible mess, as if a storm had hit it, and Alexander's usually perfectly-starched shirt now looked wrinkled.

Alexander turned around to look at Alaina and she felt as if she had been hit by a cannon ball with the wind knocked out of her. She had seen fury on Alexander's face before, and she recognized the tightening of the jaw instantly, but never had its full force been directed at her before. His hand stood clenched by his side as if he wanted to hit her, as if it was taking all his concentration to control the urge.

"You're no better than the rest of them," he finally spoke with all the disgust he felt for her evident in his voice.

"I don't understand...."

Quietly and very slowly he added, "Next time, choose someone other than your bodyguard. He can't do his job, and it leaves the door open for intruders." He turned and walked out the door without looking back.

Alaina tried to breathe, but felt she couldn't. She didn't know just what had happened, but she knew that Alexander thought she had betrayed him somehow.

She had to think. Had Mike not left and laid down in Alexander's bed, waiting for her? Had Alexander found him there and thought they were sleeping together in his bed?! Alaina couldn't stand any longer, her knees gave out. She sat on the bed, shaking.

Alexander thinks she'd betrayed him with Mike!

She had to explain. She dressed quickly and called for a cab. He had to be at the office.

She rode to the office, but he wasn't there. She had no idea where to look and New York was too big to start searching. Instead, she went back to Alexander's apartment with a heavy heart and packed her clothes together. She checked back into the Plaza. She couldn't stay in Alexander's apartment, not until she had talked to him, and she was determined to talk to him, no matter how long it would take. He had finally starting opening up to her and she was not going to allow him to close up again. But where could he be?

# Chapter 13

"We have more problems, Alexander." Rich's voice at the other end of the phone sounded tired. "We've have two more bomb threats and now we have a note saying some of the pharmaceuticals coming out of the new Medco Division have been tainted."

"Did they specify which brand?"

"No."

"Pull it all off the shelves. Send an alert to all the stores nationwide through the distributors."

"This isn't going to look good."

"Get on it right away."

Maxwell Enterprises' stocks were losing ground for the first time. Alexander knew the threats were originating from Mustafa, knew he was out to break him, but he couldn't prove it, and since the incident in Italy, no one had been able to apprehend the malefactors.

Alexander ignored the television in his study and began making some notes for the investigation he would lead tomorrow regarding the bomb threats, when he heard his name.

"New York's own Alexander McClyde, President and CEO of Maxwell Enterprises, Inc., and still one of the most eligible bachelors in America today, brought Alaina Johansson to this country, some say kidnapped, some say rescued, we have no details of this, but maybe tonight will answer some of our questions as to their connection...."

Alexander, otherwise immune to the press and their way of making a story out of any woman he spoke with, became angrier with every passing second. Now that the company stocks weren't doing well, the press would hound anyone that might have an answer. Yet, she meant nothing to him, he told himself, not after that night....

His thoughts were once again interrupted as the camera zoomed in on Alaina, and he unconsciously held his breath. The press had found her with Martha at Junior's eating cheesecake. She was more beautiful than ever. Her hair was softly curled into her face and it looked shorter, more sophisticated. Even though it had only been two months since he had seen her standing in his apartment dripping wet, it seemed much longer.

"How does it feel to be on national television?" Georgina Ford, a major network spokeswoman asked Alaina.

"I'm a little surprised," she replied, smiling.

He hadn't seen it before, but now that he had distanced himself emotionally from her, he could see it more clearly, the style and poise that was there, the composure and refinement, more self-assurance and elegance. The lost child was gone. When had that happened? Had she grown up since coming to New York, or was it just that he had always treated her as a child, and therefore she had seemed young to him?

More general conversation between the two continued and then the question was asked, "What about your love life? Is there anyone special in your life? Being one of the richest young women in America today, many young men out there would like to know."

"There are a few very special people in my life."

"So now the question all New York and probably much of the country would like to know, What is your relationship to the man who brought you to this country?"

"He saved my life, and I am in his debt always. I would do anything to return the favor."

"Well, maybe you can help him in the future. I'm told you are extremely wealthy yourself. Any plans for the future?"

"I'm not quite sure."

"Your foster grandparents died and left you quite a substantial amount of money. Can you tell us about that?"

Alaina took a deep breath, blinked a few times and said, "No, I have no comments on that."

"Thank you so much for your time," Georgina said to Alaina.

She should never have done the interview, Alexander thought. While he was in the desert she had been on his mind constantly. Then came the pang of guilt when he saw how upset Alaina had been at the question about her grandparents. He should have been the one to have told her what happened.

But he didn't have much time to think about it; the phone rang again and he found himself on the way back to the office, knowing it would be a while before he saw his bed again.

Martha read Alaina the next morning's review from the newspaper over the phone. "You're a smash!" she repeated happily. "Go out and get a paper."

"Oh Martha, please," Alaina said wearily. "You know I only care about getting a message across to Alexander, if he even watched the news, that I want to talk to him. He won't answer my phone calls, but maybe he'll be angry enough at me to call me now."

"Come on, be a sport."

"OK, hold on." She put the phone down and opened her door to get her copy of the morning paper. She opened it up and sucked in her breath. The front page news read, "More Threats Against Maxwell Enterprises." She quickly read the article and then the follow-up article on the inside of the paper. Somehow the previous news had escaped her knowledge, and now she grew concerned. She heard Martha yelling through the phone for her to pick up. "I'm sorry Martha. I was just reading the story about Maxwell Enterprises. What is going on?"

"I'm not sure. I know ever since he came back from Saudi with you strange things have been happening. Bomb threats and now this drug tainting."

"Let me call you back, Martha." Alaina said softly. A sick feeling was starting in her stomach.

She sat wearily down on the couch. Heavy strings pulled at her heart. Was she the cause of all that was happening to Maxwell Enterprises? Was Mustafa behind these attacks?

A man from the United States government had called her only a few days ago to inform her that her foster grandparents had been killed and that they would help her receive the money that was due her, minus taxes. She had wondered, in her sorrow, if it had been Mustafa who had killed them, but the man gave no further information. He probably didn't know himself, or at least, he sounded uninformed. Mustafa would know how to get revenge on Devon Maxwell also. Would Devon Maxwell loose his company because of her? Alaina understood how much the company meant to Alexander; he couldn't lose it because of her.

Alaina called Martha back and asked, "Will Devon Maxwell pull out his money?"

"I think Alexander will find a way around the situation. He always has in the past and so many jobs are riding on his decisions. He has put too much time, energy and his own blood into the company to see it go under or be taken over now."

Alaina watched the news that evening and turned the volume up when she heard Maxwell Enterprises' stocks had fallen drastically. The announcer said, "Seems as if the man with the golden touch has lost it. With retail stores threatened, people aren't shopping, and with this latest pharmaceutical poisoning, the shelves are being emptied of products, so this, his latest acquisition, is turning sour. People are afraid to keep their investment in Maxwell Enterprises. We're all anxious to see where it bottoms out and how long this man can survive. It is said that Devon Maxwell's wealth is enormous, no one knows for sure how much money he really has, but no company can continue to take the beating it has the last two weeks and continue...."

Alaina had to do something.

She called the television station she was watching.

Alexander was discussing financial options with Rich, who had flown in from Italy. "We've got some major cash flow problems, Alexander. What are we going to do?

Alexander ran his hands through his thick hair in a gesture of exasperation. "I won't lose it all. Somehow there's got to be an answer." He started pacing the room again as the drink on the counter grew warm from neglect.

"We could call in some favors," Rich volunteered.

"We need big money for the banks to feel secure."

"What about Alaina? She would lend you the funds. I heard her interview on television last night. She says she owes you."

"I won't ask her." Alexander maintained stubbornly. He had thought about the option himself, but could not bring himself to realize it might be his only way.

Rich watched his friend pace several more times up and down the room. "Not on speaking terms?"

Alexander stopped and stared at his friend. Even Rich was not privileged to question his personal life. But he realized this was different, this was business.

"When I came back from Saudi this last trip after Abdul and his family were killed, I wanted Alaina safe and married. When I found her in bed with the new bodyguard, I didn't care anymore. The old family bond is gone. My grandfather is dead and so are Abdul and his daughter. There are no more ties. She means nothing to me."

"Is that why you have a tail on her, to protect her everywhere she goes?"

"She, unfortunately, is caught in the middle between Mustafa and my family. I feel responsible."

"So marry her," Rich said emotionlessly.

"I won't marry her for money or feelings of responsibility."

"You'll never marry out of love either, you old fool. No one can live up to your standards. Alaina's the kindest, most decent girl you've ever met, and you know it. You're just too afraid to admit that someone has finally gotten under your skin, because then you'd have to admit that maybe you could love someone, and become vulnerable like the rest of us."

Alexander took a step forward, fist clenched, the muscle in his jaw twitching, but Rich remained aloof, and Alexander's anger dissipated. He turned and faced the window.

"Does she know about your other identities?"

"No."

"If you plan it just right, you could keep the marriage in name only, if you really don't love her. She could marry Devon Maxwell and never know it's you."

Maybe it was time he married again. No one except a few people knew that Alexander and Devon were the same person, and there was no reason for Alaina to ever find out. He hardly ever traveled to the ranch any more, and she could live there. She would be safe on the ranch and he knew his mother would like the company.

No, he would not do that to her.

The phone rang and Rich answered it. As he hung up the phone, he said, "You might want to turn on the ten o'clock news on Channel 6," Rich said. "Ms. Johansson's ears must have been tingling."

When Alexander didn't make a move to turn on the television, Rich did. "I want to see this."

As the camera focused in on a close-up shot of Alaina in the studio of Channel 6, Alexander couldn't help noticing that although she was dressed in a dress that covered her from her neck down to the middle of her incredibly long legs, she managed to look more sensuous than most women trying to show off every inch of their flesh.

"What is the name of your company going to be?"

"Shaded Sands."

"And you're starting with perfumes? Why?"

"My upbringing, I imagine. I miss some of the wonderful scents from home."

"How much money do you have, Ms. Johansson?"

"Too much to count," she said with a breathtakingly beautiful smile that made the middle-aged male reporter stop for a moment.

Alexander stood up and started pacing. "This is totally out of character," he said, irritated. "We have talked about privacy."

"What about Alexander McClyde? You have been seen with him on numerous occasions, but not recently. Was there a break-up?"

"Why, Alexander and I are practically related," Alaina said.

Alexander stood still and looked at the beaming face in the camera. "What is she up to?"

The reporter continued. "So you would not be the reason for the rumors of a hostile takeover of Maxwell Enterprises?"

"Hostile takeover? I think not. You see, Devon Maxwell is a very private man, and so is Alexander, but sometimes privacy can be a bad thing. I don't know why they haven't said anything with the stocks dropping so low, but they're smart men, and know what they are doing. Maybe they have plans with the stocks being so low, but there's not going to be a takeover. Devon Maxwell and I are engaged to be married. With my millions..."

"Married?" The reporter's mouth gaped open for a moment, his astonishment mirroring Alexander's.

Alexander could hear Rich in the background, and what started as a chuckle, turned into outright laughter when the interview concluded.

"Well, Alexander. You're cornered now. Confirm her statement and watch stock prices soar to new heights, or deny the whole thing and watch this whole company go down the drain."

# Chapter 14

Alaina decided on arrival that she loved Wyoming. Now, as she slid off her horse and stood for the longest time watching the awakening sky explode into brilliant, shimmering colors, she inhaled deeply the beauty of the spectacle before her and smelled the fresh scents of the grass beneath her boots. She looked down, feeling as if the earth was beckoning her, and quickly pulled off her boots and socks, laughing as she started running across the meadow, her limbs long and graceful as she squeezed the damp grass beneath her toes and felt the sun shine down on her and warm her soul.

She stopped at a small river and dipped her feet into the crisp, cold water.

She couldn't resist. She pulled her jeans off, dropped them to the ground, and waded in up to her hips, laughing as the cold water made her legs tingle and her toes numb. Even though it was early March, they had had record high temperatures since she arrived two days ago. While the air was warm, the water was near freezing.

This is where she felt at peace. No wonder Devon Maxwell lived here on the ranch most of the time.

But the thought of Devon reminded her of the

upcoming wedding and some of her happiness left. Less than two weeks after the television interview, she had come to Wyoming to be married to Devon Maxwell. Tomorrow, no less.

She knew she was marrying this man because he needed the money, and also for the lasting friendship between the two families. She consoled herself that, at least, she would be related to Alexander and maybe they could be friends, but deep down she knew that would be impossible. It was with a sad heart she waded back onto shore and to her waiting horse, Lady.

She felt a shifting wind and looked up. Far in the distance she saw a figure on a large black horse. For a brief moment she thought Alexander had come for her! But then she knew Alexander had come for the wedding. Of course he would come to his own cousin's wedding. If she could only talk to him, explain. But for some reason, he wouldn't let her. He had closed the book on them when it seemed he was just opening it. It was hopeless.

The pain was so intense at this moment that she hoped he would be going back to New York as soon as the wedding was over, so she could get on with getting over him and making Devon a good wife.

She couldn't stand it any more, being so close yet so far away. She ran to her horse, jumped on its bare back and galloped off towards the ranch, the endless tears drying in the wind.

Another sleepless night in the large house made the night drag on unbearably. When the first rays of light entered Alaina's room, they brought relief that tomorrow was finally here.

Breakfast was brought up to her room by a maid named Clara, who had given her a looking over ever since she arrived. But she couldn't eat anything this morning and instead got dressed. It was a morning wedding and she could hear guests already arriving. She had been told Devon was out of town on business and would arrive last night, so even Devon Maxwell would be a surprise on her wedding day. But it was just as well to Alaina. She wouldn't have formed any opinions about him and it made it slightly easier to go through with the marriage.

Alaina looked at her reflection in the mirror and straightened a small wrinkle in the taffeta material gracefully flowing over her hips and down to the floor. But she wasn't really seeing herself. All she saw in the reflection was a shell, void of feelings, and terribly numb.

Alaina heard a door open and looked in the mirror at Devon's mother smiling at her.

"You look radiant, my dear," she said softly, and, coming closer, put her arm around Alaina's slender waist.

Alaina smiled weakly, and, to avoid her questioning eyes, asked her to help with the buttons on the back of her gown. She felt as if she was cheating this wonderful, sweet woman out of a happy bride for her son. She had met her three days ago at the airport, but they really hadn't had much time to talk since Susan was busy with the short notice wedding preparations. It was just as well since Alaina felt guilty for not feeling the least amount of happiness over her wedding.

"Is everything all right? Is there something I can do, Alaina?"

Alaina knew Susan could read the sorrow in her eyes, but wanting to misinterpret how she meant her question, Alaina nodded and said firmly, "Tell them I'm ready."

Devon Maxwell had not come up to see her. Maybe he thought she would run away from him, maybe he was too scared. But none of that mattered to Alaina. She had made her decision.

Alaina walked out of the door with Susan, but waited at the top of the stairs where she could view part of the downstairs but remain unnoticed.

She saw Susan hesitate for a moment, as if to say something, but then sadly nod and leave to tell the piano player to start. Susan walked down the aisle with Ned, the foreman, and Alaina watched all the smiling faces Susan had probably known all her life. Alaina would not disappoint the people downstairs, nor ignore her mother's dying wishes. It was meant to be.

She walked down the stairs slowly, head held high, hearing the hush over the group gathered.

Then she stopped. Could her eyes be betraying her?

Alexander stood down below in a black dinner coat. Alone. She couldn't take this anymore. Her resolve to marry Devon was crumbling by the minute. She was about to turn and run away forever, when she saw Alexander smile and put his hand out to her. It was a smile she knew all too well, one that both mocked and applauded her, affirmed and disputed his feelings for her, and worse, made her feel both breathless and wanton all over.

Somehow she made the journey to him and reached out and clasped his hand. She felt far away, on a magic carpet, for this really couldn't be happening. She had lost Alexander, yet here they were getting married....

"Miss Johansson?" A voice penetrated Alaina's thoughts. "Miss Johansson?" It was the judge.

"Yes?"

"Do you take this man to be your lawfully wedded husband?"

She looked into Alexander's eyes and saw that he was daring her to answer anything other than affirmative. "Yes."

"Then repeat after me: I, Alaina Susanna Johansson, take this man to be my lawfully wedded husband." She repeated the words and the rest of the vows softly.

Now it was Alexander's turn and in a clear, strong voice, he said the words "I do."

"Then repeat after me please: I, Devon..." She heard no more. Was he just standing in for Devon? Was this a marriage by proxy?!

"Yes, yes," he said giving the judge a quick look of impatience and the nervous judge pronounced them husband and wife.

Alaina knew now that Alexander could not love her, not even have the slightest positive feelings for her, to lead her on the way he had and then coldly stand in for his cousin, in some sort of proxy wedding. Why? To make sure she would go through with the marriage by tricking her? She brought up her hand and slapped it across Alexander's face with such force it would have leveled a smaller man. She picked up her skirts and ran up the aisle, tears forming quickly in her eyes.

The guests gasped. Then to their surprise, Devon Alexander McClyde smiled, then burst out laughing, as he walked up the aisle after her.

# Chapter 15

Many hours after the ceremony and after the last guest had left, Alaina sat alone in a small back kitchen. The door opened and she watched as Susan startled at realizing someone was sitting at the only table in the kitchen. "Alaina!"

"I'm sorry if I scared you," she said softly, "I didn't know where to go to be alone. Back in Arabia, the men never came into the kitchen, and neither has anyone come in here, until now."

"This is not the main kitchen. We don't usually use this one. Alexander has been looking for you and I don't remember him ever being so upset at not finding someone." Susan sat down in the chair next to Alaina. "I've been told I'm good at listening. I'm sorry we haven't had a chance to get to know each other, or even talk much for that matter. But now we'll have lots of time to get acquainted." She patted Alaina's hand. "What's going on between you two?"

Alaina didn't know how to answer that question.

"Would you like to talk about Alexander?"

Alaina heard compassion and acceptance in her voice. Here was a woman who had borne much over the years and Alaina felt that she would understand. "Do you know Alexander very well?"

Susan smiled sadly, "I sometimes think not very well at all. Ever since he was very young, he had to learn to rely on himself, and I fear he's built a wall around himself that I can't seem to break down anymore."

"Can you tell me about when he was young?" Alaina asked, placing her hand on Susan's, and then almost pleadingly inquired, "and about Michelle?"

"Alexander told you about her?" Susan seemed ill at ease.

"Yes, I mean, no." She stood up and walked to the large window. "When he was sick once, he spoke of Michelle, and his father."

"Would you like to see where Alexander grew up?"

Alaina nodded gratefully; now maybe she'd understand more about this man whom she had grown to love, yet would not love her back.

The man who had married her to another.

Alaina followed Susan through the back of the house to a Jeep, and gathering her full wedding gown, jumped in with her. She looked at Susan, who was also still in her evening dress, and thought how comical they must look to anyone who saw them. Susan caught her smile and asked, "What's so funny?"

"I was just thinking we look quite unsuited for this Jeep."

Susan laughed with her. "You're right, it must look strange, but this Jeep will get us anywhere. This is the West. It's still quite wild and I like it that way. I wouldn't trade it for the hustle and bustle of the city for anything. There's the cabin, straight ahead," Susan said, pointing. "That's where I usually stay. You can come down and visit me whenever you like, the door's always open. I know how lonely that big house can get," she added regretfully.

As they entered the small log cabin home, Susan got the fire going, and Alaina felt the feeling of home. Susan excused herself, saying she was going to change into something more comfortable, and told Alaina to make herself at home.

Over the mantle, Alaina saw a picture of a little boy riding on a large work horse. She took the picture down and ran her finger over it, smiling at the little boy with a great, wonderful, genuine smile on his small face.

"That's my favorite," Susan said as she returned. "You love him, don't you?"

Alaina was shocked to hear that question asked so understandingly from Devon's mother.

"You can't fool me, young lady. I know you were mad at him today, though I don't understand exactly why, but you had love written all over your face when you looked at that photograph."

Alaina sat down on the wood floor in front of the open fireplace, not caring if it ruined her outrageously expensive dress. Her shoulders shook with the sobs that raked through her body. "But he doesn't love me!"

Susan came and sat next to her. "I think you're wrong," she whispered. "I think he loves you a great deal, even if he doesn't know it himself yet. Give him a little time, and he'll see it. He needs to know he can trust you."

"What good is it now? Time has run out. I'm now married to Devon Maxwell, whom I've never seen and it seems doesn't want to see me, a man who wouldn't even come to his own wedding."

"Look at me, child. What do you mean, you've never seen Devon?"

Alaina saw astonishment in her eyes and nodded sadly, wiping away her tears, "I know you must think me crazy for going through with it without ever having seen or met your son."

Susan frowned and asked, "Why did you marry Devon?"

"My mother wished it before she died and Devon saved my life when I was little, so I owe my life to him. If he had not wanted to marry me, I could have..." Alaina couldn't tell Devon's mother she would rather have married Alexander. "I will try to be a good wife to your son."

"What do you know about Devon?"

"Not much."

"And what has Alexander told you about himself?"

"Nothing, really. I know at some point he went to Arabia and that's why he has the stallion, and I know he represents Devon in all business transactions. I also learned that he's had many affairs with many beautiful women around the world." Alaina saw the disapproving look on Susan's face, "He didn't tell me that, I've heard about them."

"Yes, women seem to throw themselves at him, but he's never been serious about any of them."

"What about Michelle?"

"Let me put another log on the fire and get us something to drink. Why don't you get comfortable on the couch? This will take a while."

When she came back, she settled in with Alaina on the couch. "Now before I go on, I want to tell you about my son's childhood," Susan said.

"When he was sixteen, he had what we thought was a crush on a very young and pretty little Italian girl he had met while at boarding school in Switzerland. He flew her and her father here to the ranch to meet the family, and told everyone they would marry as soon as they were old enough.

We soon realized it was more than infatuation. Then not even a month later, the girl disappeared with her family and no one knew where. A letter finally arrived later from Switzerland, explaining that her father had thought it best she marry an old family friend, someone more in the same social circle and background, feeling it would make for a happier and longer-lasting marriage. That was the first blow. Then, upon my father's death only three years later, Devon's father cashed in as many stocks and CD's as he could and disappeared one night, and no one has seen him since. So you see, his father betrayed him, also."

"I'm so very sorry for all of you," Alaina said.

"It's all right now. The problem was, though, when he disappeared, it didn't leave us with much money left to run the ranch, and it's expensive. Devon, not knowing what was happening because he was away at school that year, had just married a girl named Michelle. He was very young, barely twenty, and she was twenty-one. He brought her home when school was out two months after they eloped, and was faced with the tragedy of learning that his father had squandered his inheritance. But he could have dealt with that alone. It seemed Michelle had only married him for the money, and when the money was gone, she no longer wanted anything to do with Devon."

Susan drank down her scotch in one swig. "I don't know what exactly Devon saw in this girl. I guess she was alluring in a worldly way and she knew how to get what she wanted. Devon thought he was in love again. Even when she said she was leaving him, he told her he would get the money back somehow for her, but she just laughed in his face. She wanted a divorce, she said. Devon said he wouldn't give her one since they were expecting a baby. That's when I understood why they had married in such a hurry." Susan stopped, a pained look entering her eyes. "And the baby..." Susan stopped.

"What happened to the baby?" Alaina asked.

"Devon slowly started to open his eyes to her true character over the next month, and finally agreed to divorce her, after the baby was born. She was furious for the next few weeks. She decided she couldn't wait the five months of pregnancy...and then there was an accident. It was all a horrible mistake. I remember that night too well. Devon was beside himself with worry over the child. We rushed her to the hospital. She was bleeding and of course there was little hope of saving the baby." Susan's voice became hoarse. "But the tragedy didn't end there, for you see, Michelle also died the next day, the doctor couldn't stop the internal bleeding. For some reason, perhaps guilt or realizing she wasn't going to survive, she confessed to Devon that the child wasn't his, it belonged to another.

"My son just shut down emotionally after that. He worked as a machine; nothing mattered to him but the rebuilding of his grandfather's financial empire. He escaped into the business."

"What a tragic story; no wonder he's in hiding from people now," Alaina reflected. "Anyone that's been hurt and deceived as much as that wouldn't trust anyone anymore."

"I'm glad you understand, Alaina. Maxwell Enterprises started out with one important commodity, a horse named Pegasus."

Alaina inhaled slightly. She was finally getting the whole picture.

Susan continued, "The stallion was sent to the States, and was entered in any race available to him. He quickly made millions in prize money and stud fees, and eventually earned back all the money my husband had taken, and much more. My son has a gift for making money grow. Unfortunately, along with this gift comes a penalty, that of loss of privacy."

"That's where Alexander comes in, right?"

Susan looked sadly at Alaina and sighed deeply. "Alaina, I don't know what is going on, or why Alexander has done this, I'm sure he has his reasons, and I don't think I should be the one to tell you...."

"You're right, mother," Alexander said as he entered through the door, "you shouldn't be the one to tell her."

Alaina looked from Alexander, who she could tell was none-too-pleased with her for disappearing, to Susan, who looked as angry as Alexander. It suddenly occurred to Alaina that he had called Susan his mother. She looked at Alexander in horror. "You're brothers?"

Susan spoke up before Alexander could say anything. "Do you know why this child went ahead with this marriage? To honor the wish of her dead mother, to continue a family bond that spans two continents and even to save your hide. Oh yes, I've been reading the New York papers. Could you not find it in your heart to trust her? Not every woman is a Michelle."

Alaina looked in wonder at this petite woman who dared bring up the most hated name to Alexander. She expected him to rage at her, but instead he looked intently at Alaina "I have a confession to make, one that I'm not proud of, but something I would not change had I to do it over."

Susan went to Alaina, took both hands into her own, and then hugged her fiercely. "I know we shall become great friends. Try to understand him and think of what I've told you about his life," she said, and then left the cabin.

"Why don't we sit down?" he offered.

"I think I'd rather stand," she said coolly.

"Alaina," he said, not taking a step closer to her, "I confess I hadn't intended to tell you this for a long time. I think I got some sense knocked into me," he said with a tilted smile, holding his hand up to his cheek where she had slapped him. "Devon and I are one and the same. My birth name is Devon Alexander Maxwell."

Alaina starred blankly at him.

He tried to explain, "After Michelle died and everything else was lost, I went to Arabia, I needed to get away from my life." Still, she just watched him. He sighed and continued, "When I finally captured and tamed the stallion, it was Mustafa's own father who changed the stallion's name from Aswad to Pegasus, and then referred to me as Alexander."

"As in the legend," Alaina whispered.

"It also happened to be my middle name, so after returning to the States and making my millions, Devon went into seclusion, having learned from the experience with Michelle and others that to be known as being rich was a serious drawback. Earlier, after my father left us, I legally changed my name to Alexander McClyde, after my grandfather."

"Why wouldn't people have recognized you as the same person?"

"Because when I was younger I was never in the public eye much. I already had this concept in mind on my trip home from Arabia. Rich, a young hand at the ranch, was a good jockey, and Marty, our trainer, took Pegasus to all the races. All business transactions were via telex and fax. Public appearances were not even requested at that stage in the game."

"That's what this is all to you, a game?" Alaina asked, looking into the blazing fire, instead of Alexander.

Alexander could understand her reactions, having felt them himself before—a victim of deception. She was numb at this moment to emotions, and he only now realized to what extent he had hurt her. He stepped forward, but Alaina put her hand up to stop him.

"This entire time you have allowed me to believe that Devon was this recluse to the world, a man I had met when I was a small child and built dreams around, dreams that were shattered when I met you. Why, when you knew that I loved you?"

"Loved? Alaina, it came as a total shock to me that your mother had told you that I was going to marry you. I had no intention of marrying anyone, especially a young women who thought she was in love with an idol of her youth. I could never have measured up to your childhood expectations. And then there's my grandfather, who paid off a young woman's father when I was sixteen to disappear from my life so that I could fulfill his fantasy that Abdul's family and mine would someday be joined by marriage. I made a vow I would have nothing to do with that."

"Why did my mother call you Devon?" she asked suddenly, the misery plainly showing in her eyes.

"Your grandfather would probably not have spoken to your mother much about me after she married and moved away. There would never have been a reason to."

Alexander could not bear her great sadness. He reached for her, but she turned to face him then, and asked in a voice with a chill as cold as an Arctic wind, "Why did you marry me?"

He did not touch her, but stood very close to her, his eyes very soft and filled with love, "Because I grew to love you. I wanted to deny it, telling myself only fools love, but I couldn't get you out of my mind. You were there when I woke up in the mornings, and at night when I tried to sleep. During my trips out of the country and in these past few weeks, life without you has been torture."

"What would you have done had you not fallen in love with me? How long would you have let me wait before you released me from my family's wishes to marry Devon?"

Alexander's heart sank at the tone in her voice. He had played the game and in the end, lost more than he had ever bargained for. "I would have answered as soon as you were settled into your new life in New York."

"Well, Devon Alexander Maxwell McClyde, whoever you are, I have followed my mother's and family's wishes and married you. Whatever they saw in you that they thought would bring me happiness, I will never know." Then, taking a deep breath, she announced, "Your company is safe now, and I feel no more obligation to you. Now I want an annulment, or whatever it is you do in America." Alaina noticed he took a protective step backwards at the impact of her words. "Now, if you'll excuse me, I'll ride back to the house to pack my things."

Alexander watched her leave, taking his heart with her. He rested his forehead on his outstretched arm resting on the mantle and looked into the fire, as he always did when he felt drained and searching for answers.

His whole life seemed to flash before him and he began to reflect on the things that had never bothered him before; the reputation he had acquired in the business world and the treachery that faced him there, his acquired reputation from the international press as a playboy, his eminently cynical ways. None of it made sense anymore. Now he wondered if all of that had just cost him the only thing that truly meant anything to him. He thought about Alaina bravely walking up the aisle to marry a man she didn't know, out of loyalty to her mother's wish, and he knew he couldn't let her go ever again.

# Chapter 16

Alaina stepped outside the cabin and wondered at the stillness of the night. The cold north wind that had blown earlier had died down and Alaina decided she'd take a ride before packing her things. The barn was not far from the cabin and she mounted Lady bareback, riding swiftly at first, trying to clear her head as the wind whipped through her hair. But that didn't do much. She still felt numb and tired, without any feeling of hope.

Now her wedding dress was a hopeless mess around her. She should have changed first before galloping across the countryside, but she hadn't wanted to talk to anyone at the house.

She slowed Lady to a trot and Lady whinnied wildly, shaking her head. "What's the matter, girl?" she asked looking straight ahead in the direction of the mare's fearful eyes. She saw nothing but whiteness. "Oh no," she whispered, knowing that was not sand, but snow.

"We've got to seek shelter," she said turning Lady around, but before she could, the whiteness surrounded her along with extreme cold. She couldn't see anything and her body quickly became chilled. As the cold northwest wind whirled around them, she wished for the warm breezes of

Arabia and the soft sands of the desert. At least there she'd still had her dreams intact, while here there was only cold reality.

"Lady, we have to find our way back!" she shouted over the blustering wind and snow that turned the world completely white around her. She didn't know north from south any more. "Go home, Lady, where it's warm," she said in Arabic.

Alaina lay low over Lady's neck, trying to absorb as much heat from the mare's body as possible, yet her whole body remained stiff with cold. No more than twenty minutes later, she could no longer feel her hands and her body stopped shaking. She didn't know what was happening to her and the next hour seemed an eternity.

She wondered how long she could stay on her horse, for the desire for sleep became overpowering. She had to sleep—nothing else mattered anymore. She didn't even feel cold any more.

Eternity passed. Then, from nowhere, she felt someone shaking her, yelling in her ear, and forcing her to walk. "Alaina, you have to walk!" she heard a familiar voice dictate to her, and she smiled in her daze. She knew that voice. Only Alexander bossed her around like that. Her smile quickly disappeared as pain surged through every one of her veins, every fiber in her body hurting as she started to move. He repeated his command in Arabic and it seemed forever that she was forced to walk, but he was by her side continually, his jacket around her, bracing her as he forced her to keep moving.

"I hurt," she moaned finally.

"That's good," Alexander said, "that means the blood is moving through your body again." He picked her up then and carried her in his arms. "We're almost there, sweetheart," he said tenderly in her ear.

Alaina didn't know where she was, nor did

she care, just as long as it was warm and she could rest. She vaguely recognized the cabin as he carried her in, put her gently down on the couch and stoked the dying fire. He quickly had it roaring again and went to her, carrying her to the rug in front of the fire. "We have to get you out of this wet dress," he said.

Alaina, feeling the warmth from the fire, wanted nothing more than to get out of her wet clothes and get warm. "I'm so cold," she said miserably.

Alexander wasted no time, easily tearing the wedding dress off her, leaving only her silk slip to dry by the fire. Then he rubbed her fingers and toes. "Can you move them at all?"

She nodded, her teeth chattering and her body shaking dreadfully. "I'll be right back," he said and came back with two wool blankets and wrapped her in them. He sat her in front of him, his legs stretched out around her, and started rubbing her arms.

"You're hurting me," she moaned.

"It'll get the blood flowing better," he insisted and continued for several painful minutes. "That storm has been brewing since last week, but hasn't been able to get over the mountains until now. It was a bad night to take a ride."

Her hand touched one of his legs accidentally and she realized he was soaked also. "You're wet," she said.

"Would you mind if I take these off?"

"When has that ever stopped you before?" she asked wearily, but admitted to herself that she had missed being this close to his magnificent masculine body as she felt the familiar heat radiating from him. She asked, "How is it you are always so warm?"

Hesitantly, she shared her blankets with him

when he sat back down beside her in his shorts. Unconsciously she pressed her body closer to his.

Alexander groaned softly as he felt her skin next to his. He wanted her more than he ever wanted anything before. He turned her around to face him. "Alaina, I love you more than I ever knew I was capable of loving anyone or anything. I was so afraid I wouldn't find you in time. When I realized you were out in that storm, I have never been so afraid of anything in my life. I have lost you twice in one day and can't stand to lose you again. You're my wife now and I don't want to lose you ever again."

Alaina didn't miss the darkening of his eyes, and wearily asked, "Whose wife? Alexander's or Devon's?"

"Alaina, I never wanted to hurt you. I've always had women surrounding me, mostly for the money and power. I even had women ask for introductions to Devon, openly telling me our relationship could continue after the money was theirs. But with you it was different right from the start—you disliked everything I stood for. You told me if Devon was anything like the Americans that visited your father, you wouldn't want to go with him either, do you remember?"

She smiled tragically, "Yes, I do. And I do understand now why you wanted to keep my finances from the press." Suddenly her voice went hoarse. "My grandparents—they're dead."

"Yes, I know Alaina. I'm very sorry. They were close friends. I will miss them."

She couldn't think about them know. "Everyone wanted to know how much money I really had, though even I don't know the total amount. I bet Devon knows," she said, light entering her melancholy eyes.

Alexander chuckled softly, happy to see her

humor was somewhat restored. Maybe all was not lost. "He hasn't checked recently," he said, pulling her head up to look deeply into her splendid eyes. "Alaina, I love you with all my heart."

Could she believe him? She suddenly stood up, taking the blankets with her. "If you love me so, why did you let me go through the agony of thinking I was marrying someone I didn't love? Was this some kind of test for me?"

"Maybe it was, Alaina. I haven't known much loyalty in my life, and maybe I needed to see how loyal you were."

"What have I done to make you mistrust me so?" she asked.

"Not you, me."

"Why did you take me to New York? Was that some kind of test also?"

He sighed. "In the beginning I wanted to keep the truth from you until you were accustomed to your new life, your new freedoms, and then see if we would be suitable for marriage to each other. I didn't want another experience like Michelle, who married me only for my money. But then, when I thought you might be loyal to your mother's wishes, I wanted to see if you would love me for who I was, not a promise to be kept, or some fantasy prince from your childhood that would be sure to disappoint you in real life. I thought that if you loved me, and then later found out I was Devon, I would know the real reason you married me. I am accustomed to knowing all the angles before I make a decision, but I still don't know all there is to know about you. Why did you marry Devon?"

She didn't answer and looked down at his callused hands. She had always wondered why his hands were so rough when he had an office job.

He continued when she remained silent. "And

I wanted you to see the city life, experience things on your own, have men fall at your feet, and do all the things women want to do."

"All those things don't matter to me, all I ever wanted was you," she said quietly.

"But did you know that when you came to New York?"

"No, but shortly thereafter. I missed you so much when you were gone. At first I wasn't sure if it was because I missed home, and you were connected with home, or because of you."

Alexander tried to fight the picture of Mike in his bed out of his mind. It wasn't fair to her, especially since he had just told her he wanted her to have men fall at her feet, and he now knew that Mike had come on false recommendations. Somehow Mustafa had infiltrated even his main office. Although he loved her deeply, a small part of him kept wanting to remember Mike, and he realized he'd never be able to trust her completely, not any more. But he didn't care at this moment, he wanted all of her.

Alaina saw the fire that leapt into his eyes and she looked away. "In New York there were men that wanted to take advantage of me, and I had to defend myself on several occasions, but that's something you've never done to me, Alexander, I've always been safe with you, I realize that now."

He moaned silently. "Don't think better of me than I am. I've made love to you in my mind a least a dozen times over the past months, but I was only torturing myself, thinking of you in my arms." He continued to stand before her, not moving any closer, yet aching to touch her.

She stood in front of the fireplace, remembering Susan's words to think about his life and what he had been through. She thought about all the times he had saved her life, even tonight. She thought of all the pain he'd had in his life, and that he had good reason not to trust anyone, and slowly her hardened heart melted.

Alexander saw the tears building in her eyes. "If you'd come closer, I'd hold you," he said very softly while his arms opened to her.

She tried to think about all the reasons she shouldn't, but her heart wouldn't let her. She stepped into his arms. "I'm so sorry," he whispered stroking her hair and holding her tighter, "so terribly sorry." Her body started shaking with sobs in his arms and it hurt his heart to know he was the cause. "Please, Alaina, please stop. I can't bear that I've made you this unhappy."

He held her tighter and she raised her arms around his neck and her breasts pressed against his bare chest. He reached his hands behind her back and stroked her gently at first and as he trailed his hands down her body he reached her buttocks and gently, but firmly held them and pressed her entire body against him. She didn't pull away and if she was afraid of his arousal, she didn't let on.

He kissed her again, more passionately this time, and brought one hand up to hold her breast. Again, she didn't pull away. Instead he felt the nipple stiffen beneath his hand and he moaned deeply, his kisses becoming more intense.

She felt as if she were melting into him, becoming part of him, but she wanted more, it was as if she wanted to be under his skin, a part of his body.

Gently he laid her down on the fur in front of the fire and removed her slip and soon they both lay next to each other, skin on skin. As she felt his hard and muscular body next to hers, she became slightly fearful of what was to come, yet anxious to know what more there was.

The next hour was filled with feelings that overwhelmed Alaina. She felt his touch and shivered in places she never knew were sensitive. Her body reacted on its own for him, and she never knew she could feel so wonderful. For a while, she thought she would die if something didn't release inside of her, but Alexander knew exactly what to do. It was a storm building, lightning crackling, and finally the waves crashed on the shore.

Only once had he hesitated, when she had let out a small cry at the feel of virgin skin tearing. He had stopped instantly and hoarsely whispered, as if in pain himself, "Oh, sweetheart." But she had quickly forgotten the pain and needed only what he could give her.

Later, as they both felt contented, he rolled her over him, so that she lay on top of him, and held her dearly to him. Alaina lay with her head on his chest and moments later, was asleep. He kissed her closed eyelids and whispered, "You are unquestionably loyal and kind, long-suffering and truly wonderful. I don't deserve you." Then he added ever so softly and even more humbly, "Please forgive me."

A short while later, he felt her sigh and became aware of the dying fire. He untangled himself and got up to throw more logs onto the fire. He got it roaring again and crackling with heat. He turned to see if she had awakened from the sounds and saw her staring at his back. He sighed; he had forgotten the scars marring his back. He lay down next to her, facing her.

"Let me see," Alaina pleaded.

He hesitated, but did as she asked. And waited. Other women had either gasped outright at the horrible scars across his broad back, or they were strangely turned on by them. But nothing prepared him for Alaina's reaction. She slowly, and very gently, started kissing each and every scar, as if to take away the pain that had been afflicted upon him.

She did not ask how he got the scars, but as she continued to kiss them, Alexander remembered the beating in the desert and being left to die as the sand embedded itself into his wounds. But there was no pain in the memory today; she was taking it all away. He turned around and took her into his arms, holding her tightly against him, wanting to make love to her again and again, but taking her tenderly into consideration and instead they slept, content in each other's arms.

Finally towards morning, the cold Nordic wind came howling against the window and Alexander awakened. Alaina stirred as he held her more closely to him, and then he pulled her on top of his chest, into his arms. "Good morning, wife."

"I like that," she said smiling, but then looked thoughtfully at him.

Alexander tried to read her thoughts. "What's bothering you?"

"I didn't know it could be so wonderful."

"That's bothering you?"

"No," she said, sounding playfully outraged. She hesitated.

"You can tell me anything, sweetheart." He sounded so sincere, and hearing the term of endearment brought tears to her eyes.

"Did I hurt you?" he asked suddenly with great concern.

"No," she answered and sighed, not knowing how to ask, yet knowing she had to tell him now.

"Well, it's just, I was wondering if...I did it right?"

Alexander looked at her earnest appeal and he wanted to shout with happiness, but instead he softly took her chin into his hand and kissed her tenderly. "You were wonderful," he mumbled against her lips. The kiss brought all their passion to the fore again, and Alaina came to learn that she didn't have to be under him to enjoy their intimacies.

Several hours later, while they lay sated and contented in each other's arms, and as Alexander kissed Alaina's shoulder tenderly, he allowed feelings to come forward he had never experienced before. He knew this was what he had been missing in his life. This feeling of wanting to protect and to hold safe what was his.

*His*. She belonged to him.

"Do you like children?" Alaina asked softly as her hand rubbed up and down his forearm that was holding her to his chest.

"Yes, very much."

"Would you ever want children?"

"I'd like at least a dozen."

"A dozen?" she laughed, outraged. "Do you plan on starting a harem?"

"Well, we can take things slowly, one at a time." He was laughing with her now. It felt good, really good. "Are you up for dinner at the house?"

Alaina nodded. "Your mother's probably wondering what happened."

"She knew we were together by the smoke in the chimney. She was almost as worried as I was when we discovered you had gone riding with the storm coming. She likes you, you know."

"I like her too. She'll have dinner with us, won't she?"

"I'm sure, if we ask nicely."

Alaina laughed. She liked this light-hearted side to her husband.

*Husband.*

She was married to the man she loved. Her mother would have been happy with how things had turned out. Or had she known all along?

They asked Susan to join them for dinner. As they finished desert, Alexander kissed Alaina's hand tenderly.

"I'm happy to see you so happy," Susan said to her son. "Where have you decided to honeymoon?"

Alaina pulled her gaze from Alexander's, and was slightly embarrassed as he continued to stare at her. "We were talking about Ibiza. Alexander says it's a small island off the coast of Spain." She hesitantly looked back at Alexander who still had a smirk on his face. He knew he was embarrassing her. "Alexander!"

He laughed as she punched his arm and turned to his mother. "I thought we'd visit Great Uncle Adam, but first, I'd like to take Alaina to England to visit Ian."

"I'd love to see Ian! I received a letter from him right before I came out here. I haven't had a chance to show you, but he's doing very well. He's decided he likes computers."

"My uncle would love the visit. He has a beautiful home, located right over the water. When will you be leaving?" Susan asked.

Alexander looked at his bride and asked, "Would you like to leave tomorrow?"

"Can we come back to the ranch soon?" Alaina had fallen in love with everything about Alexander's home, and it was here she finally felt she belonged, something that had been missing so much of her life.

"You'd better," Susan answered for Alexander,

laughing. "I'm so happy you like it here. You won't have to stay in New York as much anymore, will you?" she asked Alexander on a more serious note.

"You'll have to ask Alaina. Anything she wants. She has all the money now."

"It's our money," she corrected him. "We're married now, in case you've forgotten."

"I hope you'll never let me forget." He started stroking her chin with his finger and Susan took it as her cue to retire for the evening.

"I'll leave you two alone," she said smiling. "But before you leave on your trip, I'd still like to give you your wedding present. It's something I've wanted to give Alexander for a very long time, but there was never a good time. He was always so busy and wouldn't have taken the time to enjoy it, anyway. Now I think he might change his mind. Let me go get it."

"Your mother's wonderful," Alaina said watching her leave.

"Like you," Alexander answered.

"Do you have other family besides your mother's uncle Adam?"

"Are you changing the subject?"

"Yes. Do you?"

"I have cousins somewhere. Uncle Adam, one could say, was wild in his day. He never married, but had several children."

"Are they taken care of?"

He found himself smiling at her again. "You don't have to worry about everyone, Alaina. He's located them all over the years."

Susan came walking back into the room with a wrapped box about the size of a bread box. "This is for both of you, now."

Alexander asked Alaina to open it, but she shook her head. It was meant for Alexander. He opened it carefully. Inside was a small scale model of a sail boat in gold. "It's beautiful, mother." Alexander let Alaina hold it.

"When Alexander was young, he loved sail boats," Susan explained to Alaina. "Especially the old large vessels sailed by pirates. He told me one night, 'One day I'm going to have my own sail boat and sail to exotic places, just like Captain Cook.'"

Alaina watched as Susan's eyes misted.

"That seems forever ago now," Susan added reflectively.

Alexander stood up and went to his mother, placing a kiss on her forehead. "Thank you, and thank you for all the stories you used to tell me about Captain Cook."

"Maybe I told you too many stories about pirates. The press certainly likes to refer to you as corporate pirate. Anyway, she's docked in Florida. She's been finished for a few years now. There has never been a good time to tell you, but it's something I've always wanted to give you." She put her hand on Alexander's forearm. "Take the time and enjoy your life now. You've worked so hard. I used to think you were running from all the pain in you life. It's time you gave me grandchildren!"

Alexander looked profoundly at Alaina. "I think we're working on it."

Later that evening, as they lay in each other's arms, Alaina couldn't hold back the tears. Alexander misinterpreting her tears, looked worried at her, but she shook her head. "I'm very, very happy, Alexander. The winds have changed for me again. I have a family now."

Alaina snuggled up laying her head on his warm chest and missed the worried expression in Alexander's eyes. The winds had a way of changing quickly and he consciously held her tighter to him.

# Chapter 17

"Ian, take in the sails, we'll do this under power." Alexander kept his arms around Alaina as they stood before the large steering wheel, and he sailed the *Four Winds* safely into the harbor.

Alexander smiled as he watched Ian climbing with monkey-like agility to pull in the last sail. Alaina had convinced him to take Ian along on their trip to Ibiza. The vessel was large enough with its two bedroom suites.

As Ian came ambling toward them, Alexander put an arm out to him and rested it on his shoulder.

"Are we going to visit your great uncle this evening?" Alaina asked. She still hadn't told him that she had met him before, and after the information Adam had divulged, he probably wouldn't let on, either.

"Let's wait until tomorrow, it'll be dark soon."

After they docked, they ate while watching an incredible sunset together.

"I have some studying to do," Ian informed them. He went into his cabin and turned on the stereo. It blasted through the walls and Alaina laughed at the volume.

"Bright boy," Alexander said laughing and

jumped onto the bed next to Alaina, grabbing her. She made him feel so alive. "Now about dessert..."

He could be so much fun at times and Alaina laughed loudly as he started licking her exposed stomach, but as he made his way up her body, her laughter turned into moans. When he reached her lips, he stopped and looked deeply into her eyes.

"What is it?" he asked worriedly, not understanding what he saw there.

"I have to tell you something," she began.

"OK."

"How long have we been married?"

He frowned at her. "Five weeks, one day and..." he looked at his watch, "seven hours."

She smiled. Of course he would know it to the hour. "I'm normally very regular," she hinted. When he didn't follow her, she blushed slightly and decided to try again. "You should probably start thinking about names."

*Yes, of course, her monthly cycle!* He looked at Alaina and then down to her stomach, stroking it gently. He felt overwhelmed with emotions all at once. All these feelings were so foreign to him still. It was as if he had a chance to start life over again.

When he turned to Alaina again, she was sure she saw tears in his eyes. But she didn't have time to find out since he was already kissing her with a renewed passion. This time, she knew he was giving himself entirely to her.

And she gave herself completely to him. She felt so happy, she wanted to stay on the *Four Winds* forever, never changing how they felt at this very moment.

The next morning they walked the island, passing small white row houses along streets that were incredibly narrow. Some of the walks were astoundingly steep. Alaina sighed as they neared the top of a hill, and immediately Alexander scooped her up in his arms, carrying her the rest of the way. "You shouldn't overexert yourself."

"Alexander, I'm pregnant, not ill," Alaina protested.

"You're complaining that I'm holding you close?" he teased, trying to sound upset. He set her down and pointed out his uncle's villa on the next hill.

"It looks so white and clean. I love the red roof and the white stone wall surrounding it! It's like a miniature castle!"

"I like the pool. Let's go!" Ian urged them on. His shirt was already off and his lean tan body glistened with sweat. The temperature had risen enough to make hiking uncomfortable.

When they arrived at the villa, no one was home. Alexander didn't find anything unusual about his uncle's absence. Everything looked in order and they headed for the pool. "Where could your uncle be?"

"He sometimes heads for Monaco for a few weeks at a time. He likes to go there to gamble away his earnings."

"What does he do to live in a place like this?" Ian asked, impressed with his home.

"He's a writer."

"As in book writer?" Ian asked.

Alexander nodded. "He's very good I'm told. I'm sorry I never have time to read novels. Maybe now I will take the time." He kissed Alaina's forehead and then looked at Ian, who was feeling the water with his toes. "Go ahead, Ian, jump in. I'm going in to call my office."

Alaina sat down on the edge of the pool and watched Ian swim the length of the pool. "Where did you learn how to swim?" she asked.

"I lived on a ship most of my life," he reminded her. "Come on in."

"I don't know how to swim. I was never around water."

Alexander came back out to the pool and Alaina immediately saw something was very wrong. "What happened?"

"I have to leave immediately."

"I'm going with you." Alaina said.

"No," he said firmly. "You stay here with Ian. I'm flying to Italy."

"What is going on?"

Ian had now climbed out of the water and was standing next to them. "Ian, take Alaina back to the *Four Winds*. Stay there. If I'm not back in three days, sail her to England. Hire a captain for her. Can you do that?"

Ian nodded.

"Why are you going?" Alaina asked.

He held her sweet, now fearful face between his hands. "They've taken everyone in the firm hostage. They are demanding to speak with me. Please, Alaina. You know I'd do anything for you, but please don't ask me not to go. They are my employees and their lives depend on my being there."

Alaina was startled at the wild, enraged look in his eyes and she immediately knew who was behind this. "Mustafa."

"It has to stop, Alaina. We won't have peace until it's finished. For the sake of our child, let me finish this." He pulled her into his embrace again and kissed her deeply and then, as suddenly as he started, he stopped. "Take care of her, Ian." It was a command.

"Yes, sir." Ian met his cold gaze and said, "Be careful."

Alexander nodded in acknowledgment, but was already through the front door before Alaina could say any more.

Ian and Alaina walked slowly back to the boat and Ian helped Alaina down off the dock. He jumped in after her, but froze at the sound of a click. Four men came up from below with guns aimed at their heads. They didn't speak much English nor say very much at all, but Alaina and Ian understood they were being escorted off the *Four Winds* to another vessel. There, they were tied together in a small room and left alone. Soon they felt the ship heave anchor and head out to sea.

"Are we heading where I think we are?" Ian asked softly.

Alaina could only nod. Mustafa had planned his revenge well. While Alexander was heading to Italy, they were heading towards the desert.

For three days, they traveled aboard the ship. They were allowed to walk the ship once a day and given a meager meal twice a day. Soon, they would be docking in Arabia and they would be in Mustafa's world.

Alexander negotiated for two days with the terrorists, telling them they could have what ever material means they wanted, they just had to let the people go. But the terrorists also wanted guarantees of leaving the country unharmed. Finally, on the third day, the Italian government conceded and set up helicopter transportation to a waiting jet to take them back to Arabia.

Alexander ran his hands through his thick hair as he watched the men board the helicopter and then take off without any of the hostages having been harmed. He didn't blink an eye as the Italian police shot down the helicopter less than a mile from his building.

The police escorted the frightened hostages out of the building and Alexander greeted them all, relieved they were safe. He promised he would put an end to the terrorist attacks against his company. He saw Sofia in the arms of her newlywed husband and smiled slightly; it was time to get back to his own family.

Sofia spotted Alexander. "Alexander!" she cried, running toward him. She gave him a hug and handed him a piece of paper. "I have this note from the terrorists. They told us to make sure you got it."

Alexander unfolded the note and read the cryptic message. Sofia watched as a muscle in his jaw twitched and his eyes became hard as steel. He crumbled up the note and clenched his fist. "Bastard!" he mumbled under his breath.

With long strides, he headed for the nearest police car. He shouted to the nearest police officer, "I need to get to the airport."

Sofia, who was running to keep up with him, asked, "What's wrong?"

"This was all a ploy to get me away from Alaina. If the government hadn't balked for all these days, they would have had more demands. Mustafa needed the time to get her, and by now, he has her." Then, not waiting for the police to finally get around to driving, he jumped in the seat, turned on the sirens and drove to the airport himself.

The policemen ran after him a few yards until they couldn't keep up. Sofia explained the situation to the officer in charge.

The officer shook his head. "That man deserves a break. Do you know I was here nearly the entire time and never did I see him take even a break away from the phone...And nerves of steel, he has. We're going to help out as much as we can." He got on his car radio. "I want all available cars to form an escort for police car 435 headed for the airport. We have a civilian driving, and we're going to make sure he gets to the airport in record time."

"Can you call to the airport on your radio to have the company jet ready when he arrives and clear him through airport security?" Sofia asked.

"We'll take care of it," the officer said. "I don't envy the man that crosses him."

As Alexander arrived at the airport and boarded his company jet, he went through his safety check-list on the plane and silently thanked Sofia for her foresight. He made a mental note to give her a long deserved vacation when he returned with his family.

He was cleared for take off and a few minutes later, he was airborne.

He hadn't slept much in the last three days, but the thought of Alaina in the arms of Mustafa sent an adrenaline rush through his body. He had to put an end to this life-long feud once and for all; too many lives were getting entangled in this web of malevolence.

If memory served him, he knew where it was possible to safely land this jet in the desert without an air strip. They might need the plane to escape, if he couldn't get Mustafa. He would prefer to get Alaina and Ian to safety first, then return to take care of that business.

His landing went better than expected. His only problem was that any living being was at least a night's walk through the desert. He grabbed his jacket and set out on his long walk.

He didn't get far before he was met by nomads. They had seen the plane land. They surrounded him without saying a word. He didn't say anything for some time either. If they detained him, he would take them all down if he had to. "Either you let me walk and save my wife from Mustafa, or you kill me now. But I will take some of you with me."

They exchanged words and they all nodded. One of the men stretched out his arm toward Alexander, waited for him to take his hand, and pulled him up on his horse behind him. "We will take you to where Mustafa has your wife."

Alexander didn't ask questions. He took their offer gratefully. They raced over the desert sands, cutting his trip by hours, and solving the question of where Mustafa held Alaina.

As they neared the village, the nomads stopped, allowing him to dismount. "We wish you success. Mustafa is no friend of the desert people."

As the nomads rode off, Alexander organized a plan. This was one of Alaina's great-grandfather's homes and he had been here once as a young man. He had the element of surprise on his side now. Mustafa would not be expecting him for another day at least, and surely he didn't know of the secret tunnels throughout the house. He silently made his way to the other side of the village, coming in through the secret corral, hoping it was still concealed. Everything looked as it had many years ago. The tunnel looked unused. The further he got into the house, the clearer the voices became.

"What are you going to do with them?" he heard a voice ask.

"What do you care?" he heard Mustafa ask. "I don't care what happens to them. It's Alexander I want. I couldn't get him financially, but now I have something better. Do you know how long I have waited?" He heard him laugh. "Do you know how long I have waited for him to marry? Do you?" He laughed again. "And now the best part is he's married to Abdul's adopted granddaughter. What better revenge? I couldn't have planned it better."

Alexander was just on the opposite side of the fireplace now and could hear more clearly what was said. There was a pause and then he heard Mustafa lower his voice and say, "Why he finds you so beautiful I don't know, but those eyes..."

"Leave her alone!" he heard Ian shout in English. He then heard Ian moan and Alaina scream, and he clenched his fist, fighting for self-control. He told himself they were alive and right on the other side of this wall. He would have to wait until they all left the room, he needed the element of surprise. Fortunately, he didn't have to wait very long.

"Take the woman to my room. Before I kill Alexander, I want to see his face when I take what is his, as he took what was ours years ago."

Alexander checked his gun. There was no negotiating now. He heard Alaina cry out as someone dragged her from the room, and he winced. "Hang on, sweetheart," he said softly.

Mustafa spoke again, this time giving orders. "You, watch the boy, and you make sure the guards are posted. Alexander should be here by morning. Nothing can go wrong this time." Alexander heard him walk away.

He didn't have much time now. He silently entered the other side of the fireplace and quickly knocked the man that was guarding Ian on the head with his gun before the man could call out an alarm.

"Ian," Alexander whispered, patting his face to wake him.

Ian came to with a start. "Ian, take this gun and hide it under your jacket. If the men come back, pretend to be asleep. If they hear Mustafa calling from the other room, shoot as many as you can." He didn't wait for an answer. He was already looking for Alaina.

He soon heard Alaina's scream and a vicious laugh, and knew he had found the right room. He rammed his shoulder into the door, nearly breaking it into pieces. A cry of rage bellowed from him as he saw Alaina standing with her hands tied behind her back, her blouse ripped from her shoulders, exposing her full breasts.

Alexander saw Mustafa grab for his gun on the dresser as he jumped him. Mustafa fell short of the gun, but had time to pull out his knife and slash Alexander's chest. Blood quickly covered his shirt and Mustafa sneered. But Mustafa miscalculated Alexander's burning rage and Alexander jumped him, knocking him to the ground. They wrestled on the floor. Alexander grabbed Mustafa's hand and smashed it into the floor several times until the knife went flying.

Alaina saw the knife land a few feet from her. She watched the two men fighting and knew she had to do something. She had to help her husband. She quickly moved over to where the knife lay and bent down, grabbing the knife with her fingers. She didn't feel any pain as the sharp blade cut her fingers. All she could think about was getting free and helping Alexander.

She cut through the rope that held her hands bound together just as the two men stood up. Mustafa was standing with his back towards her, but Alaina knew he had somehow gotten the gun. It was no longer on the dresser and it wasn't in Alexander's hands.

Alexander stood perfectly still, waiting for a moment of hesitation when he could knock the gun out of Mustafa's hand. But Mustafa was not the usual opponent and it gave him a slight advantage over Alexander.

Before Alexander had a chance to strike or

Mustafa had a chance to fire, Mustafa found his own knife stabbed into his back and he screamed in rage. He turned around and saw Alaina backing up slightly. She hadn't expected him to stay on his feet.

Mustafa yelled in rage again and then unexpectedly kicked Alaina with all his might and sent her flying backwards against the wall.

Something snapped in Alexander. He ripped the knife out of Mustafa's back and lifted it, about to plunge it through his heart when Mustafa sank to his knees.

Mustafa turned and glared at Alaina with a look of total disbelief on his face. "You!" he said hoarsely and fell forwards.

Alexander checked for a pulse. Finding none, he grabbed the gun, jumped up and ran toward Alaina, who now lay motionless on the ground. He gathered her into his arms and quickly ran to find Ian. He was still sitting on the ground waiting for the men to return.

"Ian, come on."

Ian followed Alexander through the secret door in the fireplace and heard someone shouting just as the door closed behind him. "They won't be able to find the way in. Just keep close to me and keep the gun ready."

They exited the tunnel, ran through the corral and made their ascent over the ridge. As they walked across the top they were met by the same nomads who had dropped Alexander off.

"You have what you came for?" one of the nomads asked. Alexander nodded. "We will escort you to your plane."

They gave him two horses. Ian mounted one and Alexander held Alaina in front of him on the other.

Swiftly they rode toward the plane. Some of

Mustafa's men had followed them, until they spotted the group of nomads riding with Alexander. With Mustafa, their leader, dead, they did not pursue.

Alaina did not wake up during their ride. As they entered the jet, Alexander laid her on the jet's only couch, asking Ian to hold her head in his lap.

When Alexander had the plane in the air, he put it on auto pilot and came to check on Alaina.

He stopped instantly. For a moment, as he saw Ian with tears running down his face leaning over Alaina, he thought his own life was over. She couldn't leave him now. He couldn't go on without her. He sank down on his knees next to them. Ian looked with anguished eyes at Alexander. "It's all my fault. I didn't protect her."

Alexander felt for a pulse in her slender neck and almost crumbled with relief as he felt one. "You did what you could, Ian," he said gently. Then more sternly, "Get some cold wash cloths from the bathroom and wash her face. She's burning with fever. She might come around if we can get her temperature down." When Ian came back with the wash cloths, Alexander went back in the cockpit. He got down on his knees and prayed. He hadn't prayed since he was a child, but now he felt entirely helpless. He didn't believe God would listen to anything he asked for, he didn't deserve anything, but this was different, it was for Alaina.

"Alexander?" Ian asked and Alexander barely registered his presence. "It's Alaina. She's asking for you."

"Thank you!" Ian heard Alexander mumble as he got up.

Alexander reached the couch and knelt over her. "Sweetheart, everything will be all right. We made it." She nodded. "Does anything hurt?" She nodded again, and fell asleep.

"Keep doing what you're doing. Keep her cool. We should be approaching the airport in Rome in another hour. I'll call ahead for a chopper to get her to the hospital."

One hour later they were in a helicopter heading for the hospital. The hospital staff cleaned up Alexander's chest wound, recommending that it should have stitches, but he shook them off. He wouldn't leave Alaina's side for even a minute.

"She's going to make it," they kept telling Alexander, trying to console him.

He wouldn't leave her side during her examination either, though they tried. The resident physician was unfamiliar with her situation and asked if she was pregnant.

Alexander nodded.

The doctor looked grim. He informed him she was hemorrhaging. "From the bruise that's forming, I assume she's been struck in the stomach." Alexander, sick with worry, did not catch the accusation in the doctor's voice.

"Yes," Alexander confirmed.

"We need to do a DNC."

"What does that mean? Will that hurt her?"

"Not more than she's already gone through, I should think, but we won't be able to save the baby."

Alexander grabbed the doctor by the collar and lifted him slightly off the floor. "You hurt her and I'll..." Alexander saw the fear immediately in the doctor's eyes and put him down. "I'm sorry. I haven't slept much lately and...."

"Yes, well, I'll have to ask you to leave."

"I'm staying." His eyes locked with the doctor's and the doctor didn't voice any further objections.

Alexander held her hand through the entire procedure, but she never woke up.

When he was sure Alaina was out of danger,

and everyone had left them, Alexander cried for the first time in many years for their lost child. He would have to be strong later when Alaina woke up and he would have to tell her the baby they both wanted so much wasn't going to be...ever.

The doctors told him she shouldn't ever become pregnant again.

# Chapter 18

Alaina awakened twenty hours later. Slowly, memories came back. The days on the ship, Mustafa's ugly face glaring at her right before he died, the terrible pain in her stomach and, most painful, Alexander crying by her bed as she heard the doctors telling him she could never have more children.

During the next few days, as she grew stronger, Alexander watched her with a worried eye. The sparkle in her was gone and she never mentioned what had happened. Alexander tried to talk about it several times with her, to comfort her, but she always interrupted him, changing the subject.

A few nights after her release from the hospital, Alexander took her down to the docks, believing it might cheer her up. He'd had the *Four Winds* sailed to Italy, in hopes that Alaina would want to sail it across the Atlantic with him, back to New York.

She hesitated at boarding, but then took his hand and followed him down. She slowly walked around on deck before going below and entering the forward cabin, which had been their suite. Here, she had happily told him she was pregnant with his baby.

Now that could never be. She could have lived without having children herself, but when she had heard Alexander cry, her heart had broken.

She looked at the bed for a while and then sat down, feeling the comforter with her hand, smoothing it out, remembering their laughter. But now it was all different. It was over. She could never give Alexander the family he wanted, no, she corrected herself, he needed. He deserved that.

He came and sat down beside her. "What's going on in that head of yours?" he asked.

She looked him in the eyes and said, "I want a divorce."

Alexander stopped breathing for a moment. If she had driven a knife through his heart, she couldn't have hurt him more than with her words. Without having to think, he answered with the only answer he would give her, "I won't give you one."

She saw the stubbornness in the set of his jaw and sighed. Didn't he know it was for his own good? She stood up. "You will eventually. I'll make you see it's the best for us."

He grabbed her arm as she started walking out of the cabin. "Don't you dare walk out on me," he threatened. "Not after I've given you my heart." He was yelling now. "Don't do this!" He felt as if all sanity was leaving him.

"Please, you're hurting me," she cried as she tried to free her arm.

He let go instantly. Suddenly, understanding came to his eyes and he knew he could deal with this. Alaina was being her altruistic self again. "This is about the baby, isn't it?" She didn't answer. "It's all right, sweetheart."

"That's a lie!" she cried. He was shaking his head at her and she felt suppressed tears building in her eyes. "I heard you cry beside my bed when the doctor told you I couldn't have another baby. You've had so much pain in your life...." She couldn't continue, her body was shaking with sobs.

Alexander grabbed her by the shoulders and shook her gently, then held her tightly to him, then pulled her away and shook her again. He wanted to strangle her for being so selfless, yet hold her and never let her ago at the same time. "Alaina, listen carefully to me. You are the best thing that's ever happened to me, and if you leave me, I will die inside. There might be a shell left on the outside, but the inside would be dead. You are my life."

She still had a determined look in her eyes and he fought the sick feeling of desolation. For the first time in his life, he pleaded. "Please, Alaina. Please, don't leave me."

Alaina couldn't bear his pain another time. This man had endured so much and yet, here she was the one making him hurt. She couldn't bear it. She made one last attempt. "But what about children? Your dozen?"

"We'll adopt if you want. It doesn't matter. All that matters is that we have each other." He pulled her close to him again and let her cry heart-wrenching sobs into his chest. "And who knows, they've sent men to the moon, maybe one day men can have babies."

She laughed through her tears and said, "Men couldn't stand the pain."

Alexander handed her a handkerchief and joy made his heart skip a few times as he saw the sparkle back in her eyes. He knew he had won. Everything was going to be all right. He would make her forget all the suffering and pain she had endured. They would be together. He would cook her candle-lit dinners and hold her in his arms as they danced in the moonlight, he would discuss philosophy and religion with her, he would go horseback riding and plant flowers with her...he would grow old with her. And he knew he could trust her with all his heart, including his past.

"There is a part of my past you don't know about. It's something no one knows about except Rich."

Alaina waited as he hesitated, anticipating his telling her about his undercover adventures, but nothing prepared her for his next words. "I have a son."

"Where is he?" was the first of many questions that came to her mind.

"He's in California right now."

"Why have I never seen him?"

"Like I said, no one except Rich knows. He doesn't either."

"He doesn't know who his father is?" Suddenly she became angry. "Why haven't you told him? If I'd had a father out there and he never told me...."

"He has a father. He has a step father that he believes is his true father. I don't want to break that up. He's been happy."

"Who is the mother?" Suddenly she felt a jealousy towards the woman who had given him a child when she couldn't.

"She died many years ago. Let's take a walk and I'll tell you all about it." They walked up on the dock and then strolled along the beach as he told her the story of Rebecca. "We were very much in love and I never knew she was pregnant. My grandfather paid her father one million dollars to make sure we never saw each other again."

"When did you find out you had a son?"

"After I returned from Arabia and started making money, a lot of money. At first it seemed gratifying, but there was always something missing.

I'll admit there were women, nothing serious, but I always wondered about Rebecca. The more money I had, the more I saw its power and how easily it could corrupt. I wondered if Rebecca was happy and if she truly had been forced to disappear. I don't think I loved her any more then, but it was a nagging feeling inside. Had she tried to reach me, or run away? Maybe she had been loyal to me. I needed loyalty from someone more than I needed love from anyone. By the time I finally tracked her down, I discovered she had died in a car accident. But I also found out she had had a son only seven months after the last time we were together. I knew he was mine."

"You didn't contact him then?"

"Other things came up and it took another year before I contacted his step father. I learned they had a good relationship, and he, to my initial disappointment, was a decent man. He explained that he had loved Rebecca very much, though he felt she had always been sad. He knew the child wasn't his, but he loved him as his own. I felt sorry for this man, who had loved and wasn't loved in return, since I had experienced that. I couldn't take away from him the only thing he cared about. So I observed from a distance that my son was happy and well adjusted. He was eight then, and I knew I couldn't give him a better home."

Alaina stopped to hug her husband. "If I had known this when I first met you, I would never have doubted your helping Ian."

He kissed her nose. Alaina could see sorrow in his eyes.

"You miss him?"

"I see him, unknown to him, several times a year when I drop by on campus. I've also recently learned his step-father has cancer."

"But you could help him deal with that."

"I could hurt him more by entering his life. No, I'll help him in other ways. I have had him introduced to people I feel are important for him to know and learn skills I feel he needs in life to survive."

"But his father is ill. Will he survive?"

"I'm not sure."

"If he doesn't survive, you must let him know who you are. For my sake, if not your own, and for his. I know what it feels like to have no blood relatives."

"I'll think about it. But in the meantime, I trust you will not tell my mother or anyone else." It was not a question and Alaina did not feel insulted. It was a very deep painful part of his past she was happy she finally understood. Would he ever tell her everything?

"Can we go home?" Alaina asked, feeling safe once again.

"Where is home?"

"Ubi bene ibi patria."

He took her in his arms and said, "Let's go!"

# Epilogue

## 1995

Alexander watched as Alaina's long legs gracefully carried her up the stairs of the manor toward him. He never could get enough of her. She was smiling and her eyes were sparkling. He was wondering what mischief she had gotten into this time. "Did you find anymore stray animals today?" he asked, returning her smile.

Her heart beat faster as it always did when he smiled at her like that. "No," she said, shaking her head and laughing.

"Let's see, you took up scuba diving?"

"No," she said giggling. "I'm still working on swimming."

"I give up."

"Remember when you told me that if they could send men to the moon, then men might be able to have babies one day?"

"I might have said that."

"Well, they did send men to the moon, right?"

"Unless it was all a fake and done with trick cameras."

She saw his eyes gleaming and she knew he was teasing her. "Right?" she insisted.

"Yes, they sent men to the moon, and now

you're going to tell me you've found a man willing to volunteer to be the first man to have a baby?" He was still smiling at her.

"No, but they've found a safe way for women who couldn't have babies before to have one."

He suddenly became serious. As the meaning of the words sank into his mind, he felt as if someone had knocked his knees out from under him. "No!" he said, his voice becoming suddenly hoarse. "You will not try it. I won't let anything happen to you!"

"It's too late!" Alaina replied happily.

"No!" he repeated, shouting so it echoed throughout the manor.

Susan came running from the kitchen. "What's wrong?" she asked.

"Nothing's wrong," Alaina replied happily. "You're going to be a grandmother."

Susan looked as if she didn't know what to say for a moment, and then raced up the stairs to hug her daughter-in-law. "Are you sure it's safe for you?" she asked, worried as the initial surprise wore off.

"They'll have to monitor the pregnancy closely, but they say it should be quite safe." Alaina looked up at Alexander. He was still staring at her with an angry glare that would have scared anyone else off. But not Alaina. She put her hands on her hips and faced him squarely. "You'd better stop glaring at me like that. You had a part in all of this too, you know." She climbed a few more steps to stand next to him.

She held a bag, reached into it and pulled out a fairy tale book. "Do you remember?" She noticed his hesitation. "Do you remember the poem you wrote in it?" She saw recognition in his eyes. "I want you to write it in this book."

"And start the whole thing over again?"

"Oh no. If it's a girl, she's allowed to adore her father, and if it's a boy...."

She put her hand on his arm and smiled lovingly into his ice cold eyes, watching as they warmed under her radiant smile. "Don't do this to me," he murmured weakly, but then picked up the laughing woman in his arms, spinning her and holding her tightly to him. "I love you," he whispered into her luxurious hair.

"Not as much as I love you," she teased.

"Are we going to start that again?" he asked with mock threat.

She nodded, still laughing, and he carried her off into their bedroom to find out who was right this time.

Several hours later, as they lay content in each others arms, Alexander said softly. "Alaina, promise me, no more secrets. I've lived with too many in my life."

He was asking her if she had anymore secrets? She smiled. He had been quite open with her over the last three years. He had told her about her cousins in Sweden and why he had let her believe they were dead. They had flown to Sweden to visit them last year and to Alaina's great joy, they had received her as family. She continued to call and correspond with them and had made plans for them to fly out next month for a visit to the ranch. But he had not divulged all his secrets. "You mean you have no more secrets?" she asked innocently.

He shook his head. "You know all about my past. And I have an appointment to meet my son in New York next week."

"I'm glad. But does that mean his stepfather...."

"I'm afraid so. He's the one that called me. It's

time. Everything is coming together. I have nothing more to hide from."

"I have no secrets from you," she said. "You have no more secrets from me?"

He looked slightly confused at her persistence, but shook his head.

She touched his lips with her mouth and said softly, "I love you anyway...Lucky."

## About The Author

The author, writing under the pen name Samantha Kingsley, was born in southern Germany and grew up in Gothenburg, Sweden. While going through school, she took on a variety of part-time jobs; from working with Marine Biologists stationed off the coast of Sweden, to working in the Information and Tourist Offices of Gothenburg.

After obtaining her degree in business, she first worked for an export firm in Germany building chemical plants in Arab countries.

She met her husband in the U.S. and presently owns a house in Florida and in Michigan where she continues to write.